DATE			

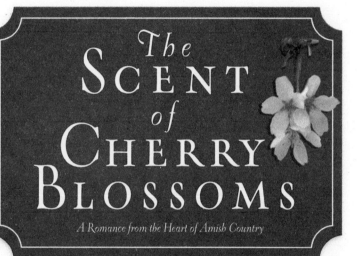

The SCENT of CHERRY BLOSSOMS

A Romance from the Heart of Amish Country

CINDY WOODSMALL

WATERBROOK
PRESS

THE SCENT OF CHERRY BLOSSOMS
PUBLISHED BY WATERBROOK PRESS
12265 Oracle Boulevard, Suite 200
Colorado Springs, Colorado 80921

ISBN 978-0-307-44655-8
ISBN 978-0-307-72963-7 (electronic)

Cover design by Kelly L. Howard

Published in the United States by WaterBrook Multnomah, an imprint of the Crown Publishing Group, a division of Random House Inc., New York.

WATERBROOK and its deer colophon are registered trademarks of Random House Inc.

Library of Congress Cataloging-in-Publication Data
Woodsmall, Cindy.
  The scent of cherry blossoms : a romance from the heart of Amish country / Cindy Woodsmall.
    p. cm.
  ISBN 978-0-307-44655-8 (hardback) — ISBN 978-0-307-72963-7 (electronic)
  1. Amish women—Fiction. 2. Amish—Fiction. I. Title.
  PS3623.O678S24 2012
  813'.6—dc23
                          2011045226

Fic.

Printed in the United States of America
2012—First Edition

10 9 8 7 6 5 4 3 2 1

One

*A*nnie added several lemons to the basket on the scale. "You have a little over two pounds."

"*As gut.*" The gray-haired Amish woman smiled. "*Ya,* as gut."

Annie wasn't as skilled with Pennsylvania Dutch as she'd like to be, but she definitely understood the phrase "yes, that's good." Her family had once known the Pennsylvania Dutch language well, but it had faded in the Martin home like a patch of sun-bleached wallpaper.

She'd been raised in a Plain home. Her clothing, with the flowery prints on her dress and apron and the circular prayer *Kapp,* was different from that of the woman standing in front of her, but Plain nonetheless. Annie's cape dress and white head covering indicated she was one of the horse-and-buggy Mennonites. They were also called Old Order Mennonites, and unlike their Old Order Amish neighbors, Annie's group had electricity and phones inside their homes.

An overhead fluorescent light flickered and buzzed. Annie pulled a paper bag from under the counter, wrote the price on it with a permanent marker, and slid the lemons into the sack. Her brother's voice echoed through the almost-empty market, and she tried not to show her embarrassment. Working at the same market as her two loud-mouthed brothers wasn't always easy.

For any of them, she was sure.

The woman picked up a Gala apple and smelled it.

"Meh Ebbel?" Annie asked. The customer already had a sack of Red Delicious in her cart, but maybe she wanted some Galas too.

She shook her head, set the apple in its bin on top of the dwindling mound, and took the sack from Annie. *"Gross Dank."*

Annie started to respond in Pennsylvania Dutch, but when an *Englischer* woman came to the counter, she decided to speak in a language all of them knew. "You're welcome."

She turned to the Englischer woman. "May I help you?"

"Naval oranges?"

"Oh, absolutely." Annie grabbed her stepladder from its hiding spot. She'd been unable to keep up with the demand this afternoon, and her brother, who was supposed to restock her supply from the back room, hadn't been in sight for hours. She knew where he was, but she wasn't supposed to leave her stand. Besides, if she complained to him, he'd bring her less fresh produce next time and disappear for even longer periods. "I tried to get a fresh box down to fill the bin earlier today, but I was interrupted. Give me just a minute." She went up two rungs. "They are delicious, aren't they?"

The woman sniffed a kiwi. "I bought several pounds last week, and my family gobbled them up."

Foul language, followed by her brother's sarcastic laugh, rang out.

Reminding herself that customers didn't know she was related to the loudmouth, Annie climbed to the top rung of the stepladder and reached for the box of navel oranges. Why did Glen always put the heaviest boxes in the hardest places to reach? She pulled it toward her, straining to get it down from its perch without spilling anything. With the box almost in her arms, she saw an avalanche of oranges tumbling toward her face. One pelted her on the cheek. She flinched, turning her head, and was hit on the other cheek by two more oranges, but she didn't lose her grip on the box itself. The few other loose oranges fell to the floor.

Glad the Englischer woman wasn't close enough to get hit and relieved she was buying oranges instead of pineapples, Annie held on tight to the crate as she made her way down the ladder. "Here we are." After setting the box on the floor, she touched her stinging cheeks, wondering how red they were. The phrase *painted woman* came to mind, and she suppressed a chuckle. How about a fruit-smacked woman? Did the Plain church frown at that?

An announcement that the market was closing came over the loudspeaker. She bagged the oranges, marked the price, and said good-bye to the woman and then began cleaning up the stand and surrounding area.

It was Saturday evening, and the market wouldn't be open to customers again until next Thursday. Annie's next day to work would be Wednesday, when all the deliveries arrived and the main prep work was accomplished. She needed to repack whatever was left in the bins and put them in the refrigerator before scrubbing down the units.

The store grew quiet except for a few employees talking to each other from their booths. A piece of loose tin on the roof rattled as the March winds howled. Winter remained shackled to the land, and Annie had long grown weary of waiting for the earth to once again tilt toward the sun.

Katie, an Amish woman at the bakery stand, asked Leah at the vegetable stand if she had any slightly aging zucchini they could use next week for making bread. Leah said she had a few.

Annie had a box of healthy but bruised fruits to take over to them in a few minutes, including the oranges that had fallen from the box to the floor. They looked fine today, but internally they had to be bruised. "Katie, I have some naval oranges to give you. They smacked me in the face before landing on the floor with a thud."

Katie continued sweeping out her stall. "Gut. They'll be good flavoring in my orange-spice pound cakes."

Whatever Annie didn't get scrubbed today could wait until she returned on Wednesday. She loved coming to work, but Wednesdays were her favorite days. Not having customers gave her uninterrupted time to prepare for the other three busy days.

After cleaning up, she carried her box of apples, oranges, and kiwis to Katie. "Here you go."

"*Denki.* Not good for eating outright, but perfect for baking." Katie put the box in a commercial-sized refrigerator. Sometimes it was hard to believe that an Old Order Amish man owned this huge, nice market and that ten years ago, before Annie lived in New York, this market was a lone stand carrying only fruits, vegetables, and a few baked goods. Now it housed four large sections—fruits, vegetables, baked goods, and meats. There were also two eateries, a florist, and a gift shop under the same roof. In the last three years, she'd worked in each one, but running the fruit stand was her favorite. By the time she went home at night, her hair, skin, and clothing smelled like a cornucopia of delicious fruits.

"I bet our driver is here." Katie removed her white baker's apron and put on her Amish black one.

Annie and four other women headed for the back room to grab their coats and bonnets from their lockers before going out the door of the loading dock. One Englischer driver brought and picked up all the horse-and-buggy Plain workers, which amounted to nine people most days. Since the morning trip started before daylight, the riders tended to be quiet and to doze during the hour drive, but on the way home, the women usually chatted and laughed about the day's events. Annie looked forward to the jokes about those oranges smacking her in the face that would make the rounds in the van this evening.

Once in the back room, she glanced through the window into the break room and saw four market workers playing cards, two of which were her brothers Glen and Eddie. Each had a cigarette in hand as he plunked money onto the center of the table. Concern and embarrassment rushed through her.

Her Amish friends, Katie and Lydia, glanced at her before looking straight ahead, probably trying not to react to the scene. Glen and Eddie made the Old Order Mennonite people look bad. Most families were very conservative, and the church's moral lines were upheld, both inside and outside the home, even if the parents had to shed their blood to do so—figuratively speaking. But Annie's *Daed* was not in the picture, and her *Mamm* was not strict, which held great appeal for Annie's brothers and tended to confuse her.

A few weeks ago a bottle of whiskey had fallen out of Glen's work locker and broken on the concrete floor, stinking up the place. Word of the incident had reached the second-story office where Jonas, the market owner, stayed. He'd called Glen to his office the next day, and the rumors were that he'd issued a warning, saying that underage drinking was absolutely not acceptable and alcohol was never allowed on the premises, regardless of a person's age. Later she'd heard Glen telling Eddie that he had apologized and Jonas had given him a second chance. Everyone at the market knew about the incident, and Annie figured the only reason Jonas gave Glen a second chance was because the market needed its few strong laborers.

She heard a card being slapped onto the table and Glen holler a curse word. Annie flinched, but she just kept walking across the loading dock and toward the door.

A mixture of disappointment and anger churned inside her as she went outside. Her wool jacket and winter bonnet were not sufficient to protect her from the howling winds that carried spatters of wet snow. She longed for the earth to warm, for budding flowers and trees to smell of sweet deliciousness, for rich, tilled soil to yield homegrown fruits and vegetables.

Moreover, she longed for Apple Ridge, where the bitter truths about her brothers' not-so-secret lives had yet to reach the ears of her people. Even when the first signs of spring did appear here, near Seneca Falls, they wouldn't be as glorious as those in Apple Ridge, Pennsylvania, where she and her family used to live. Seneca Falls had some flowering trees, but being almost two hundred miles farther north, it had nothing that compared to the blossoming of the cherry trees in her grandfather's orchard.

The five female workers sat in awkward silence while waiting on the other riders to finish for the evening. Sometimes while waiting on them, she was tempted to go help. But when Jonas gave someone a station to operate, he didn't want other workers pitching in. Each person was to handle his or her assigned duties and nothing more. After ten minutes two of the missing workers arrived, but neither Glen nor Eddie was with them.

The driver waited another ten minutes before tooting her horn. Though silence prevailed, Annie sensed the rising frustration levels inside the vehicle. She bet every person, apart from the driver, knew the holdup was that her brothers were involved in a game of cards. Except for children's card games, like Dutch Blitz or Old Maid, Plain people frowned at cards, especially betting games. It surprised her that Jonas overlooked the nonsense. Or, sitting in his second-story office at the front of the building, maybe he never knew about it. As long as people did their jobs, he rarely got involved. Her brothers played with a couple of Englischer men who had their own set of wheels. If her brothers were such good friends with the Englischer guys, why couldn't they take Glen and Eddie home?

Tina looked at Annie in the rearview mirror. "What is holding up your brothers?"

"I'll get them." Annie reluctantly got out of the van, hoping they were in a mood to cooperate. Once inside, she could see them through the break-room window. When she opened the door, smoke billowed around her. "We're ready to go. Tina is asking for you."

The four broke into laughter. "I told you she'd come for you." Ryan smirked at her.

She hated being her brothers' target, and they pulled other people into the game.

"Yeah, yeah." Glen snuffed out his cigarette. "Might as well leave. I can't manage to win one round."

Annie went back to the car, smelling of cigarette smoke and feeling like the donkey that'd had a tail pinned to it as the group applauded. She crawled into the van and stared out the window the whole way home. Her brothers reeked of stale smoke, and every so often she caught a scent of something else. Maybe alcohol? She didn't have enough experience with the smell to know for sure. Not one bit of levity or conversation passed between any of them during the long ride home.

After being dropped off, she walked across the driveway toward her house and thought she heard their phone ringing. She hurried up the sidewalk and into the house, leaving the heavy wooden door open for her brothers.

Harvey and Lorraine stood at the counter, fixing themselves a snack of peanut butter and crackers. At sixteen, Harvey was always hungry, and Lorraine, who was just two years younger, loved peanut butter more than almost any other food.

A bright lamp sat next to Mamm's sewing machine as she focused on making one of the boys a new shirt. She looked up at Annie and then at a clock. "Is it that late already?"

"It is," Annie said. "I thought I heard the phone ringing."

Lorraine licked her fingers. "Hello, Annie."

"Oh, sorry. Hi." Annie removed her coat and bonnet and hung them on hooks before going to the phone. She pressed the button to scroll through the names listed on caller ID. Her grandfather had called numerous times in the last four days, including just a few minutes ago. She'd been working at the market and hadn't spoken to him, but she assumed someone had answered his calls. Although right now she wasn't so sure.

Annie looked to Mamm, seeing only her back from this angle. "Did anybody pick up even one of these five calls from *Daadi* Moses?"

Mamm straightened her shoulders and neck as if they ached. "What, you don't think he'll call back?"

She glanced at Lorraine, who shrugged. "I was busy."

Disappointment nagged at her. Mamm's apathetic attitude seemed to be spreading like a disease, infecting all of them. Annie fidgeted with the belt to her dress. "What good does it do to belong to one of the Plain sects that allows a phone in the house if you're simply going to ignore it."

Glen and Eddie entered, smelling of fresh smoke.

Mamm turned to face her and pointed a finger at her. "If you want to quit your day job so you can answer every call from your grandfather, do so."

Annie knew she'd begun an argument without meaning to. If her devotion to God was as real as she hoped, why couldn't she manage to have one peaceful day with her mother? At nineteen years old, she should be able to hold her tongue and measure her words more carefully.

Mamm wagged her finger. "I'm both dad and mom to this family, and I don't appreciate your tone."

Annie swallowed hard, knowing her mother expected an apology. But she couldn't manage to say she was sorry. They had a phone in the house; someone should answer it! Maybe not every time, but for no one to pick up the receiver when Daadi Moses had been trying to reach them for a week? Ridiculous.

"I'll tell you what." Eddie went to the refrigerator and jerked open the door. "Next time he's sick and it's my turn to have to visit him and help out on that stinkin' chicken farm, you can go in my place."

"Very funny." For years, whenever Daadi Moses needed help and her brothers refused to go, she went in their stead, hoping her grandfather didn't pick up on the fact that they were avoiding him.

He was a good and kind man. A little strict, but what elderly Plain person wasn't? Yet, as much as she cared about him, he wasn't the only one she wanted time with in Apple Ridge.

Refusing to linger on those unwelcome emotions, she refocused on her grandfather. Occasionally he needed her to stay for an extended period to help him, but usually she went for a couple of weeks a few times each year. Her family, job, and life were here in New York, but she wanted Daadi Moses to know that she loved him.

Mamm lifted the presser foot and jerked the shirt free. "There are seven children in this household. Try not to rock the boat, Annie."

"Me?" Annie screeched. She tried counting to ten, knowing she was tired from four thirteen-hour days, and she was emotional after the embarrassment of her brothers' behavior. "I just asked a question about answering the phone. Why don't you ask Glen and Eddie how they spent their afternoon?"

Her mother looked to her sons. "What have you done this time?"

"Nothing," Glen yelled, waving his hand at Annie. "You know what she's like, Mom. All goody two shoes, like Daadi Moses."

"Glen's right." Eddie pulled the jar of orange juice out of the fridge. "We didn't do anything. We played a harmless round of cards with some friends while waiting on the rest of the workers to get done. No different than when you play Dutch Blitz with the little ones."

"Don't be ridiculous," Annie said, raising her voice. Just once couldn't her mother see past their half truths? "If that's so, then how come you make more money than me per hour but, when it's time to turn our money over to Mamm, you always give her less than me?"

"Because unlike you, we go on dates." Glen shot the words at her. "Maybe if you weren't too good for every guy around here, you'd understand that."

Mamm rolled her eyes. She'd pushed Annie to date Leon, and Annie had gone out with him to please her mother. But she didn't really enjoy his company and discouraged him from asking for more dates.

Harvey and Lorraine stopped chewing and stood there motionless and wide eyed. Annie wasn't sure where her youngest sibling was. Hopefully, Erla was out of earshot, because she hated any hint of friction, and Annie didn't want to be the cause of her little sister losing another night's sleep.

Mamm sighed. "Enough. All of you. What they do with their money is between me and them. Understand me, Annie Martin?"

Annie's body slumped, suddenly feeling heavy. "Yes ma'am." Knowing that Mamm needed help with the mounds of ironing, Annie moved to the pressing board and plugged the iron into the electrical socket. There was a time when she'd understood her Mamm, or at least she'd thought so. But now she understood nearly nothing. Placing bets on a poker game was ignored, but being kind to Daadi Moses was treated with contempt. It didn't make sense.

She wished she could sit at God's feet for an hour and ask lots of questions. How wonderful it'd be to come away with a clear understanding of what He thought and felt about all sorts of things.

Mamm brought the newly made shirt to the ironing board.

"Denki." Annie took it from her.

"You're welcome." Mamm started back toward the sewing machine. "Annie."

Annie placed the shirt on the board. Should she voice anything else or hold her tongue? She lifted her eyes, trying to get her emotions under control.

Mamm smiled, but it looked forced. "If you agree with your Daadi Moses so much more than you do with me on how I'm raising this family, maybe you should go spend a few months with him."

"What?" Annie couldn't believe her ears.

Eddie started laughing. "I like that idea!"

Mamm turned toward him, pointing her finger. "Stay out of this, Edward, or I'll send you."

But everyone in the room knew that Annie was the one in this family who didn't fit. She struggled with what the family was becoming. The more years that went by since Daed had left them, the farther they moved from cherishing each other or the Plain ways.

Eddie stormed out of the room, slamming his bedroom door behind him.

Mamm kept her back to the rest of the brood, facing only Annie. Her threat loomed over the house like a dark thundercloud.

Her other siblings watched the interaction as if frozen in place. The tension radiating within the room reminded her of the clash she'd had with her mother a year ago.

Her mother had brought in the mail, flipping through the stack of bills and stopping at a small note-sized envelope. She'd ripped it open, glanced at its contents, and then thrown a check onto the kitchen table. "Your father might as well send nothing if this is all he can scrape together. He never did bring home much, and now it's just pathetic."

Her mother's words had ripped at Annie's soul, and the hurt spilled out before she could control herself. "None of us have seen Daed in almost nine years, and the only regret you ever mention about him leaving us is that he never sends enough money. Is that *all* you miss about him?"

Her mother had stood firm, daring Annie to say one more word.

But she didn't need to. All the damage imaginable had been done in that brief exchange, and although Annie often regretted not holding her tongue when she had the chance, they'd quarreled easily and often since that day.

But right now she was just as fed up with her mother as her mother was with her. "Maybe I should."

Mamm stared at her for several moments, almost looking pleased with Annie's response. "Good. Then the decision is made."

Years of hurt pummeled Annie like pineapples falling off a top shelf, but she'd not give in to tears. No way would she give her mother the satisfaction of seeing her cry. She swallowed hard, wrestling with the fact that she'd been politely kicked out. Regret began to wind its way through her, but there would be no reasoning with Mamm at this point.

As she went to her room to pack, Annie wondered just how much she'd regret her words…and how long it would be before Mamm let her come back home.

Two

*A*den woke abruptly, as if an alarm clock had gone off. A dim glow of moonlight came in around the shades on the window.

He sat up and put his feet on the floor. The silhouette of his brother's wheelchair stood stark and empty. "R-r-roman."

His brother, in the twin bed halfway across the large room, didn't stir.

The memory of the day Roman had lost the use of his legs was never far away. Aden and Mamm were working a shift at the diner while Daed and Roman baled hay. Something spooked the three-horse and three-mule team, and they took off running, jolting Roman backward against the metal chute of the baler. Then he fell between the baler and the loading wagon. When Daed heard Roman screaming in pain, he panicked and jumped between two horses, trying to grab the reins and bring the team to a stop. Instead, he got tangled up in the rigging and was pulled under and trampled.

By the time the dust settled, two ambulances took Roman and Daed to different hospitals because of their areas of expertise. Roman had numerous injuries, the worst being the partial paralysis of his legs. He was numb below the knees, which caused his legs to easily give way if he tried using hand braces. Other injuries caused stiff muscles or spasms that prevented him from being mobile at times, especially in the mornings. Still, the doctor told him he had low-level, incomplete injuries of individual nerve cells and was one of the lucky ones who had some feeling in his thighs and knees without being in constant pain. Daed could still walk, but he'd dealt with chronic soreness ever since and was able to stay on his feet for only a couple of hours at a time.

Aden gently flung his pillow at his brother. "W-wake up."

Early morning was the one time of day this household was quiet. When he and Roman returned home from work around suppertime, the four youngest Zooks would be out of school, sounding like a barnyard of playful and hungry creatures.

Roman shifted. "Ya. Okay."

Aden lit a kerosene lantern before going into the adjoining bathroom. He turned on the shower and adjusted the nozzle toward the far wall of the oversized stall. He took his showers at night, but Roman needed them in the mornings to relax his rigid muscles. Most days, after a hot shower he could dress, get into his wheelchair on his own, and return to the bathroom to shave and brush his teeth before they left for the diner.

After putting a match to the wick of two more lamps, Aden walked to the side of his brother's bed. "R-ready?"

Roman jerked air into his lungs. "I'll never be ready for anything except sleep at three in the morning, so quit asking."

Aden chuckled and pulled back the covers. He put one arm under Roman's knees and one around his back and then lifted him out of bed. He carried his brother into the bathroom and put him on the seat in the shower, where Roman peeled out of his flannel pajamas and underwear. Aden rotated the showerhead, making sure the stream of water hit his brother just right.

Roman moaned with discomfort as he moved his shoulders in response to the hot water. Finally he drew a relaxing breath. "Ah. The only thing that feels better than this is getting your shoulders rubbed by a girl you're on a date with."

"I w-wouldn't know." Aden went to the sink and splashed hot water on his face before applying shaving cream. He'd never gone on a date. Never wanted to...except with someone he could never be with. He watched his brother's reflection in the mirror. With the exception of the wheelchair, they were outwardly identical. But their personalities had always been quite different, which used to cause a lot of friction between them.

Roman flicked water at Aden's back. "You gotta trust me about the girl thing."

Aden chuckled and ran a razor down the side of his face. "If having a g-girl is c-comparable to sitting in a wet stall during winter, I'm not impressed."

"For an artist, you sure don't see life through romantic lenses." Roman drew the bar of soap to his face. "You like the smell of soap, right?"

Aden rinsed the razor and shaved his neck. "You mean over your usual st-stench? Ya, I do."

Aden didn't hear the rest as he rinsed and dried his face. Roman was a talker, even in his sleep. Besides, Roman may have kissed a few girls in his days of dating, but all his brother really wanted was to spend evenings talking to someone special.

Before the accident, Roman had attracted young women like honeybees to nectar. Aden had never had Roman's confidence or his gift of gab that convinced girls they wanted to be around him. In fact, Aden's stutter made it impossible for him to talk anyone into anything, including a date.

Sometimes it felt as if the five years since the accident had passed in the blink of an eye. At seventeen, they'd simply enjoyed life. Oh, they'd worked hard helping their parents as needed on the farm or in the diner, but then they'd spent their money once the weekend came. Roman spent his money taking out girls. Aden spent his on art supplies and on books about how to draw. Life had a free and easy feel to it back then. And Roman had felt like a man who could conquer any challenge put before him.

But that was a lifetime ago. Only a few years had passed, but Aden and Roman were decades older than they should be at twenty-two.

"Hey," Roman bellowed. "I'm telling you important stuff here. Are you listening to me?"

"Only when I have t-to," Aden teased. "You d-done?"

"Ya."

Aden turned off the water and passed Roman a towel. "You thought any more about g-going to—"

"Ya," Roman interrupted. "And the answer is no. Uncle Ernie will have to get someone else. I can't fix generators anymore. You know that's true."

Aden shook his head. "You're j-just unsure."

"I don't lack confidence. I have absolutely no doubt that I can't do it."

"I know you c-can."

"I'd probably make things worse, cost Ernie more money, and make a fool of myself in the process."

Once his twin was reasonably dry, Aden carried him back to the bed. After putting clothes next to Roman, Aden pulled out his sketchbook and a pencil. He had only about ten minutes before he needed to feed the horse and hitch her to the rig, but these few minutes were like a fix to an addict.

While Roman dressed, Aden held the pencil loosely, hovering it over the paper. Without any idea what he'd draw, he put the soft lead against the thick page. His heart beat a little faster as his creativity began to flow. Pencil lead transformed the blank space into a horseless carriage with two faceless people inside it. Quickly making long and short strokes, he drew the finer details on the rig and landscape.

"Hey." Roman tossed Aden's pillow back onto his bed. "Do you really think I could help Uncle Ernie?"

Aden nodded and continued adding strokes to the asphalt road that meandered off the page.

"What if you're wrong?"

"I'm n-not."

"Until that generator's fixed, they'll have to hand milk each cow. I owe Ernie my help if I can give it."

"Ya."

"But this is going to be the busiest week at the diner that we've had in years. You can't get through it without me."

"N-n-not true." Aden drew the trunk of a tree, but like the faces of the people, the branches and leaves that would reveal its type remained a blank in his mind. Part of the pleasure of artwork was waiting to see what would emerge.

Roman bumped his wheelchair against Aden's bed. "Hello. Anybody home?"

Aden realized Roman had been talking to him while he drew, but he had no idea what his brother had said.

"It's time to go."

He continued drawing. "In a m-minute."

Roman thudded the rubber wheels of his chair against the bed again. "We've got too much to do to waste time here."

Aden ignored him, wishing it were a Sunday afternoon so he'd have hours to draw.

"*Kumm* on, Aden. If you're going to have pencil and paper in hand, you ought to be making lists of what we need to buy and cook."

Aden stopped and looked his brother in the eye. He had a right to steal a few moments for himself here and there.

An apology flickered through Roman's eyes, and Aden knew he could take a minute to finish. That wouldn't have happened before the accident. But Roman was independent then, and rather than wait he would have gone on by himself. His brother liked taking the lead. He knew what needed to be done, and it came naturally for him to order others around to accomplish it. Roman had never been an easygoing person, and being a paraplegic only served to agitate his impatience, but he was adapting. He had to. "Sorry. But you woke me up so we could get to work. So let's get there."

With his creative mood dampened by Roman's pushiness, Aden closed his sketchbook and tucked it under his arm. He blew out the kerosene lanterns, making the room dark again.

Roman motioned toward the bedroom door, encouraging Aden to go through it. "Gideon's coming by the diner in a few hours to get an update on how ready we are for his and Mattie's families to descend on our place tomorrow. In all the history of the Amish in Pennsylvania—maybe in all the states combined—a couple has never hired anyone to help provide meals for out-of-town guests. We can't afford to blow this, Aden. With the number of weddings that take place in the community every year, it could be a great boost to our business. But it needs to go really well. Word of mouth is important."

Aden knew all that. Roman had a habit of repeating information that everyone already knew, sometimes with the same speed and repetition as Aden made strokes on paper.

Roman followed Aden through the farmhouse, giving his brother the chance to move items out of the narrow path so the wheelchair didn't get hung up by the occasional toy or misplaced clothes.

When they entered the wider expanse of the kitchen, Roman wheeled ahead. Their Mamm stood at the stove, pouring coffee into one of two tall thermoses. As always, she was fully dressed with her hair freshly combed and pinned up and her prayer Kapp in place. No matter what life dished out during any season, she faithfully greeted the day and her children with organization and routine.

Aden and Roman would have coffee made at the diner in about thirty minutes, but she got up before sunrise Monday through Saturday to hand them a hot drink in cool weather and a cool one in hot weather.

"Morning, boys." She put the thermoses on the table.

"Mamm, tell Aden he needs me at the diner this week."

Mamm kissed Aden's cheek, a morning routine he'd long ago grown accustomed to. She looked into his eyes for a moment, strengthening him with her respect and love.

Roman sighed. "If Ernie's generator had gone out any other time than now, I'd go."

"N-not true."

Roman glared at him. "For a man of few words, you sure do say a lot." He huffed. "I'm telling you, we have too much going on."

Mamm bent and kissed Roman on the forehead. "Your uncle wouldn't have asked if he had any other way to get it fixed. I know my brother, and he must really need you."

"But the diner—"

"Your Daed and I can take shifts helping Aden for a few days. Although your three youngest siblings won't be much help, Mary may surprise you, even at thirteen."

"She's needed here at the house to help with Arie, Jake, and Benjamin," Roman protested.

Mamm put her hands on the armrests of the wheelchair, her face inches from Roman's. "You're so good with mechanical problems."

Roman shifted the wheels of his chair, causing Mamm to back away. "Was. Before the accident."

"The solution Ernie n-needs is in your brain, not your l-legs."

Roman angled his head, his brows knit tightly. Aden hoped he'd finally said something that could work its way past Roman's insecurities. "You're right. If he needed legs, you could do it."

Aden rolled his eyes, but he wouldn't swap insults with his brother or call him on it. Roman had never said it in so many words, but Aden had always believed that before the accident, Roman thought he was better than him. Aden used to find that annoying but not worth fighting over. Right now his brother needed to believe he could outdo Aden in some area, and Roman definitely liked the idea that Ernie had asked for his help instead of Aden's.

Aden wanted him to have that confidence as much as Roman did.

Roman rubbed his hand over his chin. "I would love to get my hands on an engine again, maybe prove that I still have what it takes."

"You do," Mamm assured him.

Roman glanced to his brother, fear oozing from him. In a lot of ways, Aden preferred Roman's former overinflated ego to the shards of brokenness left from being wheelchair bound.

Roman went to the pegs near the back door and grabbed his coat and hat. "I'll call Ernie as soon as we get to the diner. It'll probably be ten o'clock or later before he can find a driver who'll come all the way from Lancaster to get me."

Mamm smiled. "I'll be there by ten, then."

To be honest, Aden had no idea how he'd handle the demands facing the restaurant this week without Roman. It would've been much easier to let him go any other week. But Ernie needed him now. And pushing Roman to go was the right thing to do.

On the other hand, if Aden messed this up, no one in Apple Ridge would ever ask Zook's Diner to host meals for their out-of-town guests again. It'd be the first and last event of its kind. Mattie and Gideon might end up sorry they'd trusted Zook's to feed their families. Aden hated even considering that possibility. But how could he live with himself if he let Roman miss this chance?

Three

*E*llen scooped a shovelful of mulch onto the soil. She turned the blade into the ground, stabbing and mixing the old dirt with the new fertilizer.

The sun against her back radiated its warmth through her wool coat. It wouldn't be time to plant for another four weeks, maybe more. But every year about this time, she invited the coming spring in this manner. It was like putting out a welcome mat. She gladly received every season, knowing it brought its own special reprieve. By summer's end, after having plowed, planted, weeded, and harvested through two seasons, she'd be ready to embrace a sleeping garden and soon afterward the first snowfall.

Marriage and raising children had its seasons too. But it was getting harder for her to embrace the season they were in these days. Since the farming accident had damaged her husband's and her son's bodies, it seemed that life had moved from a home on a plot of earth that enjoyed four seasons to a shack built on frozen tundra.

But she trusted the One who'd made the very first garden. He knew how to prepare and strengthen her for life. She went to her knees, grateful for the solitude of this place. Whispering prayers for her family, she churned the dirt with her gloved hands.

The kitchen timer inside her coat pocket rang in quick succession, reminding her she could linger only a little while longer before hitching the horse to the rig. She pulled it out of her pocket and reset it for ten more minutes. Her moments with God had to draw to a close, but she wasn't quite ready yet.

Roman had gone to her brother Ernie's place yesterday, so she and her husband would help at the diner today. David had gone to work with Aden at three thirty that morning. He could stay on his feet for only short periods before the pain became intolerable, but he was hoping to last until lunchtime, when she would relieve him.

The sound of dried leaves and grass crunching caused her to study the patch of woods behind her garden. It could be someone's cat or dog moving about, but the noise had a rhythm to it, like human steps.

A young woman emerged from the trees, wearing a flowered dress and a navy-blue coat and carrying a small basket.

Annie? Ellen's heart picked up its pace. She rose to her feet, knocking dirt off the front of her black apron. She refrained from calling out to her visitor in case she was one of Annie's sisters, though they didn't visit their grandfather nearly as often as she did. But the girls did favor one another, especially at a little distance. Moses Burkholder had become a business partner of Zook's Diner before Ellen was born, and he'd been a neighbor since the day she married into the Zook family. Of his four granddaughters, Annie held a special place in Ellen's heart. But she couldn't reveal her favoritism.

The girl waved. *"Guder Marye!"*

It was Annie. Her smile could thaw a winter freeze, and an unexpected joy engulfed Ellen. Annie had come to Apple Ridge around Thanksgiving, but her grandfather had bronchitis then, and Ellen saw her for just a short visit.

Ellen hurried to the cattle gate and opened it. "Annie," she called to her. "What a nice surprise. I hope you're not in Apple Ridge because your Daadi Moses is sick."

Annie cast her eyes downward and shook her head. "No, he's well. Denki for asking."

"Gut. Then I'm even more happy you're here."

Annie lifted the basket she was carrying. "I brought you fresh eggs, a loaf of apple bread, and two jars of preserves I made when I was here last summer."

Ellen leaned in and put her cheek against Annie's, giving her a hug. "You are the sweetest thing." Then she backed away, looking Annie in the eye. Despite the girl's grin that revealed her charming dimple, Ellen saw unhappiness in her bluish-green eyes.

But they rarely talked about the things that weighed on Annie's heart. Ellen looked at the basket and decided to tease her. She clicked her tongue, mocking disgust. "Look at what you've done."

Annie angled the basket away from Ellen. "Well, if you don't like it…"

Ellen grabbed the basket. They shared a laugh while she shut the gate and then put her free arm around Annie's shoulders.

"How are you, child?"

Annie's chin trembled slightly, as if she might be trying not to cry. "By the looks of your actions, you're as eager for spring as I am."

"I'm trying to hurry it along."

"I'd be glad to help you with that."

Ellen's heart warmed. "The way you said that, I have to ask if your grandfather sent you over to give me a hand for a bit."

"He did. You know Daadi Moses. He's usually under the weather when I come here and keeps me really busy, but since he's not sick, he's got his week all lined up and has almost nothing for me to do. He said if I was being useful, I could stay until dusk. Even later if I call him first."

Ellen chuckled. "Child, you are useful to my soul even if you do nothing but keep me company."

"Denki." Tears brimmed for a moment. Then she cleared her throat and motioned toward the patch of woods. "It wasn't easy getting here. There's another fallen tree on the path."

Ellen knew Annie had faced more of an obstacle than a fallen tree to get to Apple Ridge. Based on the little bit of news that had traveled from New York to here, Ellen knew that the family had grown more dysfunctional by the year since Annie's Daed left them. And the sweet girl's mother blamed her own father, Moses, for a lot of the problems the family faced. But Ellen doubted Annie knew that or the story behind it. "Regardless of the problems, you're here now." She put her arm around the young woman's waist. "Just goes to show that fallen trees, no matter how strong they once were, can't block you from following your path."

Annie swiped a tear off her cheek. "You always say just the right thing."

This conversation reminded Ellen of who they were—unrelated neighbors who rarely talked freely about things of the heart.

After Moses's wife died, he became a single father to three-year-old Mabel. He remained a brokenhearted widower throughout Mabel's young life, and he knew precious little about raising a headstrong girl. Alarmed at the choices Mabel was making at eighteen years old, he made decisions for her and set her future in stone. A little more than two decades later, Mabel's third child, Annie, had grown into the adoring daughter Moses never had.

The kitchen timer rang out, making both of them jump. As they laughed, Ellen pulled it out of her pocket and turned it off.

"Do you want me to run into the house and get something out of the oven?"

Ellen chuckled. "This timer has nothing to do with my kitchen. I need to get to the diner."

"I can fetch the horse for you and hook her up to the carriage."

"Denki. You know…" Ellen paused, excited at the thought of having Annie's help. "We could use your help serving folks today."

"I'd love that. I haven't served tables at Zook's since I was fifteen."

Some days it seemed like an eternity since Annie had sacrificed a year of her life to help out at the restaurant while David and Roman battled their way to being able to work again. Ellen had intended never to ask for another restaurant workday from the sweet girl, but she sounded eager to go.

"We're really busy at the diner this week. A young couple from the community has relatives and friends in town for their wedding, which is taking place next week. They're using the diner to feed folks a few meals because the bride-to-be is determined to keep things as easy on her elderly parents as possible."

"Elderly parents? How old is the bride?"

"Only a few years older than you, but she was a late-in-life caboose for her parents. Anyway, between that and the fact that Roman went to my brother's place to fix a generator, we need your help."

Annie's eyes lit up. "I'll go hitch up the carriage right now, and we can be on our way in no time."

After parking the rig under the lean-to near the diner, Annie followed Ellen across the parking lot. As they went inside, the bell jangled loudly, and Annie inhaled the aroma of fried bacon and grilled hamburgers. A customer stood at a rack of gum and mints near the diner's register.

Behind the pass-through, Aden stood at the grill, quickly preparing food. Five booths were filled with people—most of them Englischers. In the private room she saw a large table partially covered with place settings. A stack of plates with a lot of flatware on it indicated that whoever began setting the table had been interrupted. She assumed that's where the Plain folks would be served when they arrived. Most of them wouldn't be used to eating at restaurants and placing orders, so food would be placed on the table family style, just like eating a meal at home. Aden once told her that's how the Amish handled meals after the church service too. Whatever she knew about the differences between the two groups—horse-and-buggy Amish and horse-and-buggy Mennonites—Aden had taught her.

His Daed crossed the restaurant, coming toward them with a pitcher of water in one hand and iced tea in the other. His long beard had turned completely gray since the last time she saw him. Beads of sweat dotted his forehead, and he walked stiffly, grimacing slightly at times.

He caught a glimpse of his wife and stopped, setting the pitchers on an empty table. "Well, hello, gorgeous. Take a seat, and I'll be sure to get your order next." He winked. "As long as I get a kiss for a tip."

Ellen giggled. "David, you remember Annie."

He looked at her. "Annie?" He frowned and turned back to his wife.

"Ya." Ellen nodded encouragingly.

"The only Annie I know should be about this tall." He held his hand four feet off the floor. "And she had her hair in braided pigtails the last time I saw her."

Annie smiled, thinking about all the times he'd joked with her by tugging on her hair and squealing like a pig. He'd seen her a few times since the accident, and she wondered if he was teasing or if he truly didn't remember. Ellen once told her that since the accident, his memory wasn't what it used to be.

"Excuse me." The man at the register waved a packet of gum in the air. "I'd like to check out."

"Sure." Ellen hurried to the register.

A call bell rang, signaling that Aden had food ready to be delivered to a table. She peered his way, hoping to see his welcoming smile, but he was too busy cooking. She returned her attention to David. He was studying the tables of folks, probably noticing the empty and almost-empty drinking glasses.

Aden rang the call bell again, setting out two more plates. David glanced at the pass-through.

"I came to help," Annie said. "Why don't I get the food on the tables. I'm better at that than serving drinks."

"Denki, Annie." He headed to the table where he'd set the pitchers of drinks when she arrived.

She hurried toward the pass-through as Aden prepared more food. Last time she came here was right after Thanksgiving when she dropped off eggs from her grandfather's chicken farm. Aden had come out of the kitchen and spoken to her briefly, but he wasn't one for words.

She picked up the ticket under the nearest plate.

Aden looked up. His eyes grew wide, and a smile slowly spread into a grin. "W-well, hello, A-Annie."

"Hi, Aden." She studied the ticket. It'd been four years since she'd waited tables at Zook's. "Are the tables numbered the same as before?"

He nodded.

"Gut." She grabbed the plates. "Now, if I can remember what that was, we'll be in good shape."

He flipped two burgers at once before glancing at her, wordlessly questioning if she was serious.

"I'm kidding." She laughed. "It's so busy in here today. Much better than the last time I stopped by."

Aden smiled and nodded. He looked as though dozens of thoughts were running through his mind, but he remained silent.

As Annie served the guests, she thought about the gentle, soft-spoken man in the kitchen. After the accident, she'd moved in with Daadi Moses, and they both had worked by Aden's side at the diner. At fifteen she became used to Aden's reluctance to talk. Whenever she came to Apple Ridge, she'd go out of her way to catch a few minutes of talking to him, not that anyone knew that—although she was pretty sure Roman suspected as much.

She looked Aden's way, seeing someone she'd never seen before. He was still Aden, and yet he wasn't. The last time they'd worked together, he'd been an awkward teen who carried the weight of his brother's and Daed's injuries and the possibility of losing the restaurant. Now, at twenty-two, he seemed to be confident of himself in that kitchen. She wondered what else about him had changed.

She was determined to find a way to break his silence—even if she had to break every dish in the joint to get him to speak up.

Four

*A*lone inside the generator room of his uncle's barn, Roman sat in his wheelchair, staring at the oversized metal box on a concrete slab. His palms sweated, and nausea rose in his throat. What was he doing here?

He rolled his chair back and forth—an inch one way, an inch the other—staring at the gray container.

He'd grown up working on this generator and had always had a knack for fixing motors. A hired mechanic had taught him the basics, and ever since graduating from school at thirteen, Roman had kept this thing running. But it'd looked a lot smaller to him before.

Before he'd lost the use of his legs.

Before his self-confidence had been mutilated and left for dead.

Before becoming neither boy nor man.

Did even Aden understand what it was like for him? In some ways he'd had more power and strength as a preteen than he did now, and the reality of that never dulled. Back then, he'd taken for granted feeling like a man. Now he took nothing for granted.

The square metal box loomed before him, daring him to think

he could accomplish something of value as he used to. Daring him to try anything these days without Aden by his side.

His uncle opened the barn door and stepped inside. "What do you think?" Ernie sounded desperate and hopeful. He had no money to replace the generator, and it'd take a team of professional mechanics to fix something this outdated.

Roman had arrived yesterday afternoon to a houseful of excited relatives who had a feast waiting for him. He'd never made it out to the barn. Today he hadn't even removed the casing yet to look at the insides, but Ernie needed to believe it was fixable as much as Roman did. "I'll have it humming like new by the end of the week."

His uncle's stiff body relaxed, like an uncooked noodle wilting in a pot of boiling water.

Ernie put his hands on Roman's shoulder. "I sure do appreciate this. No mechanic would even try to get this unit working again. I started thinking I might have to sell a few cows to pay for a new generator. But if I sold that many, I'd have a new generator to hook to the milkers but no cows to milk."

Roman eased his wheelchair forward and laid his hand on the casing, noting the sandpaper feel of the gray paint. "Bring me your toolbox, and we'll get started."

The constant hum of voices and flatware clinking against plates stirred both encouragement and anxiety in Aden. Today was Tuesday, the first day of serving Mattie's and Gideon's friends and loved ones. He had the rest of the week to get through before Roman returned. Roman was right. They knew of no other Amish couple who'd relied on a restaurant to help meet the needs of the visiting family, and it could be the last time anyone in the surrounding area ever tried using Zook's this way if he messed it up. What had he been thinking to encourage Roman to leave this week of all weeks?

He needed to get a head start on baking pies, marinating chickens, and chopping vegetables for tomorrow, not to mention seasoning forty pounds of hamburger meat and pressing it into umpteen dozen patties.

Annie brought another ticket up to the order wheel and attached it. She tucked the pencil behind her ear and leaned in. "The dupe is in. One hockey puck. One tender. Veg it double."

She was having a great time using all sorts of so-called restaurant terms that he wasn't sure were real. He enjoyed her sense of playfulness, especially as the workload increased. If he didn't stutter, he would respond with his own made-up terminology and wisecracks.

He placed two plates of food on the pass-through and jerked a ticket off the order wheel.

She grabbed the plates, compared the ticket to the food, then hurried to the right table.

Aden wasn't sure how he'd have handled today if Annie hadn't shown up. Roman usually juggled everything outside the kitchen while Aden handled everything inside it. With Roman gone, Mamm had seated people and run the register. Daed had helped as best he could until he had to leave to pick up Aden's four school-age siblings from school. Without Annie bustling food from the kitchen to the tables, there would have been a lot of unhappy customers today.

Annie came to the window. "Okay, Aden." She grinned, making the familiar dimple in her right cheek. "Baker needed for table five."

At twelve she'd been a skinny tomboy with freckles and a wayward dimple, neither of which bothered her. At fifteen she'd been self-conscious, avoiding smiling as much as possible and staying out of the sun in hopes her freckles would fade. Since then she had continued changing as she came into the diner every so often. Now, at nineteen, she was a slender beauty who seemed comfortable with herself and apparently liked to tease while working.

"A-am I b-being re-re-re-…" Aden couldn't manage to get out the word *replaced*. He could hear it smoothly in his mind, just as a speech therapist once told him to do. Aden had seen more than a few doctors and speech therapists over the years, but they hadn't been much help. Annie had asked for a baker, and he wanted to ask if he was being replaced, but all he could do was stutter. He wished he hadn't tried to speak without Roman here to talk for him. But Annie was standing there waiting patiently, so he had to finish his sentence. "…re-replaced?"

"Ah, I finally stumped you with my restaurant slang. A baker isn't a short-order cook. It's a—"

Before she could explain herself, Aden grabbed a foil-covered baked potato out of the heated sideboard and placed it on the shelf of the pass-through.

"Potato." She sounded defeated. "Fine. I didn't stump you this time. But I will. Just watch me."

He pointed at his eyes and then to hers, signaling that he would watch to see.

"Ya, I hear you." She put the potato on a plate and glanced behind him. "You need a bubble dancer." Annie picked up the plate and left.

He looked over his shoulder and saw a sink full of dishes. A bubble dancer must be a dishwasher.

Mamm carried a tub of dirty plates into the kitchen and set it beside the sink. "It's three o'clock. Annie's locking the doors."

Just as he and Roman did this time every day.

"I can't stay. There's a meeting of church leaders at our house tonight, and I haven't even cooked dinner."

"Not a p-problem." He was sure Annie would head out with her, leaving him to clean up from today's busyness and prepare for tomorrow's event. He didn't figure he'd be done before two in the morning, and even then he might not be as prepared for the day's business as he needed to be, but he'd manage somehow, as long as it gave Roman a chance to do something he really loved.

Annie came to the pass-through. "The last of the customers are ready to pay, Ellen."

"Okay." Mamm washed her hands and dried them on a towel. "I'll ring them up, and then we have to go."

Annie eyed the stack of dirty dishes and the messy work stations. "I can stay."

Mamm looked surprised, as if the idea had never crossed her

mind. And he was sure it hadn't. A single Amish man alone in a closed diner with a single Mennonite woman wouldn't be on anyone's list of wise ideas. Annie was no longer considered "his little friend," as Mamm used to refer to her.

Mamm cleared her throat, gaining her composure before she smiled. "No, dear. That's not a good idea."

"Ellen, I'm not leaving Aden with this mess. He can take me home after we're done." She angled her head. "Unless you don't want me…"

Aden had to assure her that she'd always be welcome, but it'd take him five minutes to say that, so he settled for a short, to-the-point statement. "Of c-course we d-do."

Relief eased the concern on her face. "Gut. Then it's settled."

"I'm not sure your grandfather will be happy with you staying into the night."

Annie wrinkled her nose. "Oh, stuff and nonsense, Ellen. He and I practically lived here when David and Roman were injured. Why would he mind now?"

Mamm's face twisted with emotion. She apparently didn't like this arrangement, but Aden saw no harm in it. He needed more help than his parents and siblings could give him, and Annie was available.

Aden turned off the stove. "C-call Moses and ask if he m-minds."

Mamm shook her head. "I'd rather just take her—"

Annie slapped the top of the counter and grinned playfully. "You're both walking on eggshells. I'll give him a call to let him know where I am and when I'll be home. Problem solved."

Aden could see his Mamm wasn't convinced, and he understood

her concern. As Old Order Amish, Aden's family couldn't have electricity in their home or business. But without electricity, government regulators would shut down Zook's Diner. It didn't matter that they could do everything using gas or generators. Government codes dictated that they have electricity.

As an Old Order Mennonite, their neighbor Moses Burkholder had the right under his church's authority to have electricity. So Aden's grandfather had formed a partnership with Moses years ago.

Aden was the third generation of Zooks who'd always gotten along nicely with Moses, and he'd never do anything to jeopardize their relationship. His Mamm was just being overly cautious.

Moses would have no problem with his granddaughter helping out again in their time of need, would he?

Five

*A*s stiffly as an old woman, Annie walked down the hall toward the lone glow inside an otherwise dark home. Once in the kitchen, she caught a glimpse of her grandfather at the kitchen table. She blinked, trying to keep her eyes open.

The next thing she knew the lights went out. "Better?" Daadi asked.

"Much. My eyes don't want to work this morning."

He'd pulled the cord to the glaring overhead lights, leaving only the dim radiance from the bulb over the stove. The aroma of coffee surrounded her, and the bright red numbers on the digital clock said it was seven minutes after four. She rarely went to bed as late as she had last night or got up this early, but Aden had needed her help getting desserts and breads prepared for today.

"I don't like that you came in after I was asleep. That's entirely too late." Daadi lowered the newspaper he'd been reading. "Tell me exactly why you've come to visit me." His directness was why her siblings didn't like him, but she knew his heart. Trusted in its sincerity above all others.

When she'd arrived three days ago, he'd welcomed her openly and hadn't even asked how long she planned to stay. But right now she could tell he was disappointed that she'd been out so late last night. Still, his accusing tone hurt.

She shrugged. She didn't want to put him in the middle of the bad blood between her and Mamm, so it'd be best if he thought she was here of her own free will. And she didn't want to tell him that Mamm had insisted Annie stay until Mamm decided she could return home—probably for a few weeks. Maybe for months, but Annie had brought only one suitcase of items. "You used to like it when I showed up to see your orchard of cherry trees in bloom."

"Don't play me for an old fool, Annie. Not you." His gravelly voice stood on the edge of anger.

"I needed a break from Mamm." It wasn't full disclosure, but it was the truth.

His intense expression eased somewhat. He folded the newspaper and laid it on the table. "What time did you get in last night?"

Yawning, she sat. "Aden brought me home around twelve thirty."

His nostrils flared, but the rest of his face reminded her of granite.

She reached over and patted his hand before grasping it. "I know. You don't like that I stayed out so late. I don't blame you. But like I said when I called, I was as safe as if I were here with you."

"I doubt that."

She couldn't help but chuckle. He wanted to keep her under his wing, while her mother pushed her to spread her wings. Mamm wanted her to date, if not Leon, then others, maybe even lots of others. Seemed to her that the two were as opposite as humanly possible.

"Daadi, you asked me to give Ellen a hand yesterday with whatever she needed. She wasn't doing laundry, groceries, or meals. She needed assistance at the diner."

He sighed. "Our Lord knows that, with Ellen's husband down more than he's up, she needs help whenever we can give it. But I never intended for you to leave her property yesterday."

"Roman's at his uncle's, trying to get a generator running." She explained about the diner needing to feed Mattie's and Gideon's families for various meals throughout the week. "The restaurant will be the busiest they've been in years."

"And Roman's gone."

"Exactly."

He rubbed his hand across his freshly shaven face, a habit when he was thinking deeply. Hoping he'd let this go, she got a glass out of the cabinet, went to the refrigerator, and poured some orange juice.

Daadi picked up his folded newspaper and tapped it on the table. "It's not proper for you to be in a rig with an Amish boy, especially that late at night. It'll look like you two are seeing each other."

"I didn't think about that." She took a sip of her drink. "But nobody saw us. The roads were deserted. I certainly don't want to cause any trouble for the Zooks."

"Or yourself."

"I'm not worried about that."

"You should be. Our people won't like it one iota better than his."

Some aspects of their religion made little sense to her, but she knew why she and Aden couldn't be seen together. Old Order Mennonite and Old Order Amish were good neighbors, helpful, kind, and generous, but the boundaries concerning interrelationships were wide and high and made of steel.

Unacceptable.

Inappropriate.

Forbidden.

So much so that a single woman from one group could never be alone with a single man from the other.

She didn't take this boundary as seriously as Daadi Moses and others like him did, because she believed it was based on prejudices between the two groups. Her relatives often used terms like *backwoods* to describe the Amish, while the Amish used words like *worldly* to describe the Mennonites.

But her grandfather was good to the Zooks, and they were good to him. The relationship—both business and personal—worked for both families.

She saw no reason to point out her grandfather's undercurrent of prejudice. He would argue that his convictions were founded on Scripture, and he'd have chapter and verse to back him up. If she argued with him, he might send her back to her mother...if Mamm would have her.

Besides, she'd never known anyone who wanted to cross that line and probably never would. She couldn't imagine giving up the modern-day comforts of her Mennonite community, which allowed electricity and phones in the home. She even considered a church building to be a true modern convenience, unlike the Old Order Amish, who had to move furniture out of a house in order to set up the church benches and who prepared a meal afterward, however simple, for hundreds of people. And the thought of living all summer without an air conditioner or a fan in the house was enough to keep anyone from crossing that boundary.

And Old Order Amish people who'd officially joined the faith, like Aden and Roman had, could never get their minds around the idea of leaving their Old Ways and destroying all ties to their family and community in order to have something as frivolous as electricity and a phone in their home.

Daadi Moses wagged his finger at her. "You take care, Annie. Our people will think you're up to no good if they see you out with a Zook, and his will think the same thing."

Annie cringed at her grandfather's tone of disrespect toward the Zooks, but she understood the source of it. The Amish weren't as moral in their dating practices as the Mennonites. Her people didn't believe in having a *rumschpringe,* the period of increased freedom for teens and young adults to find a spouse. Mennonites viewed those relaxed rules for the Amish young people to lead toward potential impurity. And Mennonites didn't wait until they were preparing for marriage to join their church. In fact, Mennonites had to be members of the church before they could go on a first date, and they couldn't date anyone but a fellow Mennonite. Annie liked the idea of dating only those who'd already made a commitment to God.

She enfolded his hand with hers, encouraging him to stop pointing a finger at her. "The Zooks are good people who need a helping hand. If you weren't in the middle of preparing for new chickens to arrive, you'd be helping them out with me, just like we used to do."

She wanted to tell him that she thought no more of working beside one of the Zook boys now than she did as a child, but that didn't feel completely honest. There was something different about her feelings for Aden. She wasn't interested in him as a beau. But she longed to know him better…and to help him in more ways than just serving meals at the diner.

Daadi Moses got up and brought the orange juice to the table, a peace offering of sorts. "A girl can't afford to have her reputation tarnished. If one of Aden's parents couldn't bring you home, you should've called me so I could pick you up."

"It was midnight before we finished everything that needed to be done. Ellen couldn't stay that late." She poured more juice. "And you were asleep by then."

Anger flashed through his eyes. "You and Aden were alone?"

Annie rolled her eyes. "Oh, please, Daadi. You're starting to sound like Mamm."

Confusion erased all sternness in his expression. "What do you mean?"

"She thinks every single man is a potential beau for me. It makes me sick. How many people have you wanted to live with for a lifetime?"

The tender side of him that she knew so well finally reflected in his eyes. "Only one. Your Mammi Esther."

Annie smiled. "No one in the twenty-five years before her or the forty-five years after." She pointed her finger at him, mimicking what he'd done to her earlier. "I'm no fool, Daadi. Don't treat me like I am. Not you."

Daadi eased his callused hand over hers. "What are you trying to talk me into?"

"I just want you to trust my judgment. Like you always have."

He rubbed his forehead, not looking completely convinced of his decision. "Okay. You can continue helping at the diner."

She hugged her grandpa, suddenly aware of the excitement pumping through her at the idea of spending a few days with Aden. She'd always managed to get beyond Daadi Moses's surliness and into the part of his heart where tenderness lived. Seemed reasonable to think she could figure out how to get past Aden's quietness and into the place where his thoughts flowed as freely as falling cherry blossom petals on a windy day.

Six

R oman pulled the timing chain off the top of the sprocket and
wriggled the cam with the small pry bar, trying to remove it
from the bottom of the sprocket. Most types of engines had long ago
started using timing belts, but not this one. His hands and clothes
were covered in black oil, and the air around him smelled of diesel
fuel.

Outside the small generator room, his uncle and every worker he
could hire were milking cows by hand. They all had their hopes
hung on Roman's being able to fix this ancient piece of machinery. So
did he.

His uncle had set up a worktable near Roman and had placed all
the tools on it so that no one had to stay with him to hand him the
needed items. Being unable to get items out of a toolbox that sat on
the floor or on a table of regular height made working by himself
impossible. But this setup was helpful. Earlier the tools had been lined
up neatly on the tabletop, but now they were in a pile at the corner,
where he'd laid each one after using it.

The work of his hands, mixed with the smells and sounds around him, unleashed a sense of well-being. He'd forgotten what it meant to feel like himself. He used to enjoy who he was and what his body could do. But contentment had disappeared along with the use of his legs.

Today, however, he had moments of feeling normal again, a sensation of wholeness he hadn't realized was missing. He didn't understand all that was taking place inside him, but he knew it was happening because of the pleasure and satisfaction in taking apart a broken machine and putting it back together as a working unit.

He wished someone could put his body back together again. As useless as that thinking was, he couldn't stop his mind from latching on to that hope every waking moment.

But right now a new hope was taking root, one with a smidgen of real possibility. Maybe when his sister Mary graduated from the eighth grade this spring and could then work during the day, he could get away from the restaurant long enough to take a part-time job as a generator mechanic. But he'd need Aden to travel with him so he could get around, and Aden needed him to be his mouthpiece.

They were both at a disadvantage this week, Aden more than him. Uncle Ernie's oldest son was able to help Roman get in and out of his wheelchair some. Aden had no one who knew what he was trying to say as well as Roman did.

But if something could be worked out, there was no shortage of Amish farms with generators used for numerous things, from running an air compressor for milking cows to refrigerating the milk until it could be picked up. Some Amish wives used generators to run their wringer washers. A few used them to heat the home or run their refrigerators. He felt confident there was enough work to keep him busy.

"Excuse me?" A female voice interrupted his thoughts, and he dropped the pry bar with a clang.

Roman turned the wheel of his chair to face the doorway.

A young Amish woman smiled at him. "Roman Zook?"

He picked up the cloth from his lap and wiped grime off his hands. "That's me."

She actually strutted toward him. "You don't remember me, do you?"

He studied her face and let his eyes move down her body. She was cute and feisty. "I'm pretty sure I'd remember you if we'd ever met."

Folding her arms, she narrowed her eyes. "Flirting already. Some things never change, do they?"

The way she ended her sentences with a question seemed familiar. "Marian Lee?"

"Ya."

"Good grief you've changed. Except you're still asking questions."

"Am I?"

He laughed. "You're right. Some things never change."

She was a year or two younger than he was, and being a neighbor of his uncle's, she used to come by with her parents when he was here. But he'd never been interested in her. The last time he saw her, he'd been sixteen, and she wasn't of dating age. But he remembered her folks fretting over her, saying she was as opinionated and strong willed as any man they'd ever met.

She pointed at the pry bar on the floor. He backed up his wheelchair, suddenly feeling like a clumsy toad.

She picked up the tool, then put space between them. "You stopped writing."

"It was nice of you to send me letters after the accident." And he'd answered a couple. It'd felt good to know someone cared, even somebody he barely knew. "But after the first few, I didn't have anything else to say."

"Ya, me either." She pointed the pry bar at him. "You look good."

He didn't believe her. That was just what people said whenever someone had been ill or injured. "Compared to what?"

She raised an eyebrow, sending a shiver of exhilaration down his spine. Her eyes held a challenge, as if she'd go toe-to-toe without being intimidated by him.

A man came to the doorway, carrying a bowl with a cloth over it. "Marian, I wasn't sure where you'd disappeared to."

She glanced his way before turning back to Roman. A hint of dare flickered through her eyes. "I'm right here."

Disappointment crashed in on him. The man had to be the boyfriend.

He entered the room. "Hi." He set the bowl on the table near Roman. "Marian and I came by to say a friendly hello, and your aunt told us where you'd be. She had me wait until she fixed this snack for you."

Marian held out the pry bar to Roman, keeping a firm grip on it even after he grasped it. "Like I said, you look good, and that's compared to any man your age."

Emotions skittered and sizzled like water poured on a hot engine.

"Marian." The man sounded displeased.

She released the tool before gesturing toward the man. "You remember Andrew?"

Roman blinked. "Your little brother?"

Challenge and humor danced in her eyes. "Yep."

Andrew shook his hand. "Good to see you again."

"You too."

Andrew had been a scrawny kid the last time Roman saw him. Andrew began straightening and lining up the tools on the table.

Roman laid the pry bar across his lap. "You knew exactly what I was thinking when he came into the room, didn't you?"

She shrugged, a huge possum grin on her face. "I was hoping."

"You have a cruel streak," he teased. "I'm not sure I like that."

"Then let me make it up to you."

"No thanks." Fear of this bold, interesting woman danced with the hope she stirred. What would she say if he invited her to attend a singing with him?

She brushed her fingers across her cheek, as if she'd felt a bug or something, and in the process unknowingly left grimy marks. "Afraid you won't survive my effort to make up for my rudeness?"

"Very much so."

"You're smarter than I gave you credit for, aren't you?"

"So I look good, but I also look stupid?"

She giggled, clearly enjoying their banter. "Maybe."

He tried to size her up. She had more zing than any girl he'd ever met. Was she just horsing around, or was she seriously flirting with him?

If this conversation had taken place five years ago, he'd have asked her out by now. But he didn't know enough about her to be certain what to think. Suddenly it dawned on him that she was probably acting this way to give a crippled man hope that his life with girls wasn't over. "I don't need pity."

Her laughter echoed inside the small room. She looked at her brother. "He thinks I'm capable of feeling sorry for someone."

Andrew scoffed. "Ya, and the Sahara is dairy farming country. My advice, Roman, is run."

Roman put a hand on each leg. "I can't."

She studied him, scrutinizing him with her beautiful brown eyes that were almost as dark as her hair. "You never did run after or away from any girl, did you?"

"Not that I recall." He'd never needed to run. If he was interested in someone, he'd ask to take her home from a singing, and if she said no, he never asked again. If a girl pursued him and he wasn't interested, he'd nicely tell her so—at least he hoped he was nice about it.

She looked at the gunk on her hands and frowned. "I suggest you learn how to pursue…unless you intend to give up dating for the rest of your life." She wiped her hands on her black apron. "Since I'm currently between beaus, you can practice on me."

"I'm not sure brazen women are my type."

"Gut. Because I'm not sure a wheelchair-bound man is my type."

She'd just addressed the elephant in the room, the one everyone always pretended didn't exist.

"You've got style, Marian."

"And another one bites the dust," Andrew mumbled.

Marian giggled. "Pick me up tonight around eight."

He couldn't get in or out of a carriage without someone strong to lift him. Rigs sat up high, the doors were quite narrow, and there was never room for his wheelchair. Aden had designed a buggy to carry the wheelchair on the outside of it, but that was in Apple Ridge. "Tonight?"

"Your aunt said you're planning to be in town only through Sunday at the latest."

"True, but..." That awful sense of powerlessness clutched his heart and squeezed. Determined to overcome the feeling, he came up with a different plan. "Maybe you should come by here. We could play a board game or something."

She frowned at him. "What's the problem, Roman?"

"Nothing." He couldn't confess the reality of his situation, not to someone as strong and bold as she was. If she saw him as too weak to even take her out, she'd cross him off her list of possible beaus before he knew whether he wanted a second date.

"Then pick me up at eight." She turned and walked out.

Roman glanced at her brother.

Andrew rolled his eyes. "I warned you. She'd look a dragon in the eye and dare it to ever spew fire again. The scary part is, she'd win that fight."

Roman stared at the doorway she'd just gone through. Had he ever been strong willed enough for someone like her? Back when his confidence was in place, he could charm the sweet, kind girls. But not someone like Marian. Then again, surely he could survive one date… couldn't he?

Seven

Stars twinkled brightly through the carriage window, and Annie was too restless to be taken straight home. She stole a brief glimpse of Aden as he silently pulled out of the restaurant lot. It was nearing ten o'clock, but they'd just finished the food preparations for the next day.

Their hours together preparing food for tomorrow's menu and cleaning up dirty dishes had felt more like spending time with a good friend than accomplishing a weighty task. Except during a true work frolic, the men undertook one task while the women did another, usually men building something and women tending to little ones and preparing huge meals. She liked her and Aden's method much better, interacting constantly while doing their jobs.

Did he care as much about spending time with her? Her thoughts jumped to the man her mother had been so positive was the right one for her. Leon had loved spending time with Annie, and her mother had really expected Annie to like him. For her sake, Annie had tried. For all her lack of warmth, Mamm did care about her. Annie knew she did. She sighed.

Aden slowed the rig. "S-something wrong?"

"Just thinking about my Mamm."

He nodded.

If Leon had been even a little like Aden, she might have been able to give in to Mamm's wishes. She'd gone out with him several times, hoping to learn to like him. It would have pleased her mother.

"You m-miss her?"

She shook her head. "I miss who she used to be. And I'm sure she feels the same way about me. We used to get along decently enough… before I became of dating age."

Aden gave a reassuring smile, looking as if he'd like to ask questions or talk about it, but instead he nodded and began humming. But the music wasn't a long monotone without meter or melody, so common for the Amish. It sounded a bit like the tune to "He Leadeth Me."

"*Ach,* I love that song. Would you sing a few words for me?"

He shook his head.

"Just a few. Please?"

He drew a deep breath and sang, "I have no idea what the words might be, but it's a song that sticks with me."

"You have a lovely voice. Sing again."

He made a face before smiling and singing, "I don't know what to tell you, what to say, how to move you."

She laughed. "You changed songs."

"I don't know where I heard it, but I think it's from a soundtrack to a play or a movie. We have a supplier who gives parties at the restaurant a few times a year, and he sets up a stereo during them. He used to come into the kitchen and talk about the movies he'd seen and what tunes went with what movie." Aden kept a tune going.

"Wherever that one came from, I wouldn't tell your bishop about that song if I were you. Did you hear yourself?"

"H-hear wh-what?"

"You didn't stutter over one word."

"I know," he sang, returning to the tune of "He Leadeth Me." "The doc says singing comes from a different part of the brain than talking. But you wouldn't want me to sing everything I need to say, would you?"

"I'd have you communicate in any way that makes you most likely to open up and share—whether it's stuttering, singing, or sign language."

He looked surprised. "You're very s-sweet, Annie," he half sang and half spoke. "But sign language?" He dropped the reins to the horse and gestured nonsense with his hands. "Ach! Not a good idea." He elongated the words, staying in perfect pitch.

She giggled and picked up the reins. "I'll drive; you talk."

He retrieved the reins and turned onto the long lane that led to her Daadi's *Haus.* "You talk; I'll drive," he sang.

Despite his difficulty with words, she found Aden to be everything she'd looked for in a man, and the thought terrified her. He was even-keeled, encouraging, kind, fun, and as genuine as God's deepest lake.

Annie unbuttoned her jacket. The current warm spell would make for a very pleasant walk, even this late at night. "How long has it been since you've seen the cherry tree orchard?"

Aden hummed for a moment. "Four years, almost five," he sang. "You showed it to me in full bloom the spring you turned fifteen."

"Would you like to park the rig and walk to the orchard? I want to know if there is the slightest sign of budding."

"It's d-dark."

"I'll keep you safe."

"N-no." He laughed and then sang again. "We won't be able to see the buds. But if the point is to walk and talk, I'd rather not sing to the cherry trees."

Next week when Roman returned and Mattie and Gideon were married, she'd have no reason to come to the diner to work beside Aden. These last two days had been the best she remembered having in her life, and the desire to enjoy this short bit of time outweighed her guilt for doing something behind her grandfather's back. "I'd like to see you sing to my Daadi's orchard."

"Of course you would." Despite singing those words, he clearly mocked frustration. At least she hoped he was pretending it.

He pulled off the driveway and onto the field and brought the rig to a halt.

"I wonder." Annie opened the door of the carriage. "Maybe all you need to do is think of a tune while talking."

"Maybe." He sang the word boldly, raising his head and putting his hand to his chest as if he were on a stage.

Laughing at his antics, she fell as she got out of the rig. Aden hurried around the carriage, but she got to her feet quickly. She straightened her dress and pointed a finger at him while trying to curb her giggles. "Not funny."

He chortled, all the while waving his hands in a gesture that said it wasn't funny at all.

They walked down the hill. The stars twinkled as a lone cloud crossed in front of an almost-full moon. Once near the stream, she paused, taking in the beauty of the multitude of barren trees. "Did I ever tell you why Daadi Moses planted all these trees out of sight of passersby?"

Aden shook his head.

"Daadi Moses was a farmhand for Raymond Zimmerman, and he fell in love with his eldest daughter. She wasn't old enough to date because her strict father wouldn't let her go out until she was twenty. She cried, trying to get her father to change his mind, but he wouldn't. Daadi Moses assured her he'd wait, but she didn't believe him. So he bought a cherry tree, saying that he'd wait for her for as long as that tree lived. Wanting to make it a gift to her, he asked permission from her father to plant it on his property. But the man refused." Annie grabbed a low-hanging branch and pulled it close, inspecting it for possible buds.

Aden touched her shoulder and used his index finger to signal for her to continue. Her heart warmed at the thought that he was interested in this. No one else who mattered to her seemed to care at all.

"My Daadi Moses bought one small plot of ground with a stream running through it. That piece of earth wasn't big enough to put a house on, only a few trees. He'd pass her home every Saturday on his way to the plot of land that held the tree. I guess it was a way of letting her know he was taking care of that tree. And it gave him the opportunity to put a letter in her mailbox as he passed by. Sometimes she could get away and meet him at the mailbox without her parents knowing. He said those few brief minutes had to sustain them for years."

Aden propped his hand against a tree. "I never knew any of th-this."

"Despite his persistence, the girl's father didn't budge in his decision. He even said that when she did date, she couldn't marry until he said so. Daadi Moses bought another cherry tree and planted it."

Aden gestured at all the trees. "How l-long did he wait?"

"Four years." She couldn't help but smile. "The woman was my grandmother, and he bought her a tree every year, even after they were married and for a long time after she died. Isn't that beautiful?"

"And s-sad."

"He worked long, hard hours during those years and bought all the land we can see. Whenever one of the trees dies, he plants another. They loved each other dearly, and this orchard will be a glorious testimony to that in a few weeks."

"That story d-doesn't sound like M-Moses."

"I know. He's a good man but doesn't come across as prone to sentimental actions. I like to think maybe that's what love does—reaches into the best and deepest parts of a man."

"Just a man?"

"I'm telling you my personal viewpoint, so, ya, it's about the heart of a man. It probably sounds like pure foolishness to you."

He smiled and shook his head. "Not at all."

They meandered side by side farther into the orchard. Had he noticed how much smoother his speech patterns were while they were in this field? Maybe he was thinking of tunes while talking. But she didn't care if he stuttered over every word; she loved hearing what he had to say.

"Wh-wh…" Aden stopped and then hummed a tune. "Why did he plant it out of sight?"

"Ah, I left out that part, didn't I?" The barren trees were so beautiful against the night sky. "He said it was because the love between him and Esther was hidden from passersby. It was a private thing that my grandmother's Daed could never see and never destroy."

"Sounds like M-Moses was right."

Was it like that for every couple—that the love binding them couldn't be seen or understood by passersby, even their own flesh and blood?

"And it gave them a place for picnics and long conversations once they were allowed to see each other."

Aden pointed in the distance.

She looked in that direction. "I don't see anything."

He got behind her and extended his arm over her shoulder. Her eyes followed down his coat sleeve and index finger. Two deer stood at the edge of the creek, drinking.

This place had always seemed magical to her.

She turned to Aden, studying his face and hoping she was reading him right. "You like it here too, don't you?"

His smile was enough to assure her. "Ya."

The deer jolted and ran through the orchard and across a knoll. She wanted to see Aden again, as much as time allowed. But was that wrong of her? Didn't her grandfather see her grandmother some without their parents' approval? Maybe they didn't go for walks, as she wanted to do with Aden, but they caught a few minutes at the mailbox, shared letters, and waited. Was walking through this orchard with Aden that much different? "Will you meet me here as often as we can until the trees blossom?"

"Definitely," he whispered.

She'd always cared for Aden—sometimes just as a friend, sometimes more like a crush—but right then she knew that she cared about more than his determination to communicate with her. Was she falling in love with who he was, whether speaking or silent?

Roman lay in bed, hoping the pain reliever would do its job. Trying to get into a buggy with the help of someone who wasn't his brother had resulted in a pulled back muscle.

The date had been worth it. Still, frustration stirred.

His one date in five years, and for it to go off without physical injury, he'd needed Aden to help him get around. There'd been a time when Aden relied on him—Roman had been his voice—but Roman hadn't needed his brother. Now he required Aden's help much more than his brother needed his. The whole situation was more wearisome than Roman could stand.

He'd gone to Marian's house, but he'd dealt with some physical discomfort at times throughout the evening—not that he'd told her. She should have agreed to his suggestion to come to his uncle's place. But no, she balked, and he'd caved like a man desperate to go out with a woman.

She'd been fascinating the whole evening. If he were a whole man, he'd be a match for her, a good one. More resentment stirred. He once could've moved mountains with an act of his will.

Now he couldn't move his own big toe.

Hoping the medicine would ease his pain and bring sleep, he tried to think about the good parts of tonight. Like her sassy sense of humor. And when he'd arrived in the rig, Marian had come out and climbed into it, so he didn't have to get out again until he returned to his uncle's place. But all they could do was ride and talk.

Even though they'd shared a few good laughs, he had no illusions. She'd dated him because there was no one else to go out with tonight, but she'd probably prefer being alone to going on another buggy-bound date with him.

He shouldn't have been excited about tonight. All he'd done was set himself up for more disappointment. After five years one would think he'd have learned by now.

Suddenly he missed home and working beside Aden. He ached to talk to his brother. Aden always lifted heaviness off Roman's back, and even when his brother said nothing, which was often, Roman found solace in their closeness.

His back pain eased, but no pill could relieve the ache inside him. He'd had a fleeting hope that God had a hand in Ernie's generator woes, putting him in Marian's path again. Clearly, God just wanted his uncle's generator running again so the cows could be properly milked.

Eight

Aden turned off the grill. All cooking was done for the day, but the kitchen was stacked with dirty dishes, and he looked forward to a quiet afternoon of working beside Annie.

He wiped off the work station, putting items in the pantry or refrigerator as he went. When she'd arrived around four that morning, he was tempted to give her the sketch he'd made of her and the cherry orchard. But that seemed forward. Maybe inappropriate. Would it reveal too much of his heart to her?

After their time alone, walking and talking two nights ago, his mind would not let him rest, so he'd done as he always had when trying to cope with feelings about Annie—he'd pulled out his sketch pad. He'd spent every free minute drawing with lead and colored pencils. Annie's delicate features filled half the page, and cherry trees in full bloom covered the other half. He hadn't planned the drawing to turn out that way, but the image had taken on a life of its own as he worked, making Annie appear as if the orchard were a part of her soul.

It was the best work he'd ever done—subtle yet vibrant with color and detail—but it was folded and shoved into his pants pocket like an unwanted sales receipt.

"Aden." Gideon peered into the kitchen from the pass-through. "Do you mind if Mattie and I come back there for a minute?"

Aden motioned for them. He removed his apron and set it on a nearby work station. Today was Friday, the last day the couple needed the diner to help feed their friends and family from out of town. From the start, Mattie had felt it was important for tradition's sake that she and her family take over feeding the guests in the customary style during the last three days before the wedding. Aden didn't doubt she had the energy for it. Both she and Gideon were so happy that the room could not contain their enthusiasm.

He remembered how miserable Gideon and Mattie had been after they split up three years ago. At the time, Aden thought the breakup made no sense. They had seemed crazy about each other. But they had ended their relationship, and both had moved away from Apple Ridge. Now that Aden knew the whole story, he understood. Gideon had been diagnosed with leukemia, and in his determination to free Mattie from the burden his illness would put on her, he ended their relationship. Without knowing the truth, Mattie moved to Ohio to live with her brother and began a cake shop—Mattie Cakes. And the two stayed apart for three years. After a close brush with death, Gideon began improving. Mattie's shop burned down, and after she returned to Apple Ridge, she learned the truth. And forgave Gideon.

In some odd way the story had a few similarities to him and

Annie. She'd once lived in Apple Ridge, moved away, and returned to steal his heart. The last time they worked side by side, they were simply friends. Now, almost five years later, she'd returned, and their bond grew stronger with every glance, word, and dream.

Gideon pushed the swinging door open with the palm of his hand and held it there for Mattie to go first.

Gideon's actions had been based in love, especially since he was deathly ill and in isolation for the better part of a year, but maybe relationships weren't often meant to be practical. By misleading Mattie, Gideon had caused both of them more pain. They were apart three years—almost to the day.

Mattie grinned. "I can't thank you enough for helping feed our friends and family this week so the burden of it didn't land on Mamm. I never expected the kind of service you've given us."

"Glad we c-could do it." Aden focused on a song, the music and cadence, and it seemed to help.

Gideon put his hand on Mattie's back and rubbed it. "I can't figure out how you and Annie kept all the orders straight while running both the family-style meals for us and providing for the regular customers, and you were able to serve the meals so smoothly."

"S-s-sign language, sort of."

Mattie smiled at Gideon. "We used to do that when we were kids. And when Gideon stayed at his grandmother's, we used flashlights for Morse code, spoke through walkie-talkies, and tied notes to the mane of a horse."

"Neither of us knew what the flicking on and off of the flashlight meant." Gideon chuckled. "But we'd do about anything to stay in contact, even after we'd spent the whole day together."

Annie came through the kitchen door with a bin of dirty dishes. Aden's heart turned a flip, and he understood the overwhelming need to be in touch every waking moment. But the truth was, even if Annie cared for him, as he hoped she did, they faced worse survival odds than Gideon had.

"A-Annie missed a lot of sleep to help out this week."

Mattie peered around Aden toward the sink. "Denki."

Annie unloaded the bin and rinsed her hands. "I've enjoyed every minute," she said over her shoulder before turning off the water.

Aden held out a kitchen towel, and she dried her hands. The sense of comradeship between them felt so right.

"You two are walking down the aisle next week, right?" Annie asked.

Mattie glanced up at Gideon, looking the happiest Aden had ever seen her. "Tuesday. I wish we had room for one more guest."

"Don't think a thing about it," Annie said. "These events are for family and friends. So, where will you live after the wedding?"

Mattie's eyes met Gideon's, and she chuckled. "With his grandmother. She has lots of room."

Gideon winked. "Which is exactly where we told our families we'd live when we were just little kids."

"Only then," Mattie said, "our plan was to live on separate floors of the house, me sharing a room with his grandmother. That's a change in plans I'm sure she appreciates."

"No doubt." Annie smiled.

Someone from the diner called to Gideon. "Well, we'd better tell the stragglers it's about closing time here. We just wanted to thank you both."

They left, and Aden wished Annie and he had a chance at a happily-ever-after too. But how could they? They'd each taken a vow to stay faithful to their respective churches. It was forbidden for them even to court.

Annie passed Aden the towel. "I need to get back to work."

After she left, Aden finished wiping down the work station, his mind fully on Annie. His mother was at the side door, chatting with numerous Old Order Amish women she'd known her whole life.

Aden grabbed a wire brush and began scrubbing the grill. He and Annie had enjoyed each other's company a lot over the years. During her long stay after the accident, they'd shared a special bond—working and praying together as friends during that stressful time while Daed and Roman recuperated. When they discovered they shared a similar sense of humor, they grew even closer. Every time she'd visited Apple Ridge since that time, his feelings for her had grown stronger. But he'd stood his ground, refusing to give in to the dream of what he wanted most out of life—Annie.

The bells on the diner door gave a muted jingle. He glanced up and saw Annie. His attention stayed glued to her as she held on to the doorknob while talking to Gideon and Mattie, the last customers left in the restaurant. Annie waved before she locked the door behind them.

Watching Annie made his heart feel all tingly and vibrant, as if an electric current ran through it. He and Annie would work for two more hours, and then they planned to share a meal he'd make for her. Afterward they'd go for another walk in the cherry tree orchard, this time in the daylight. They might ride horses…if they could do it without being seen.

He'd never looked forward to anything like he did having time with her.

His mother snapped her fingers, pulling his attention away from Annie. Mamm had that worried look—the one she had for a full year after Daed and Roman's accident.

"What?" He went back to his work, raking the wire brush across the grill.

"Aden," she whispered.

When she said nothing else, he looked up and saw her staring at him. She gestured toward Annie. "Please, Son, tell me I'm not seeing what I think I see." The desperation in her voice made him cringe. "Look, this doesn't seem like two old friends working together. You must know that."

He hoped and feared his mother was right.

Before he could say anything else, Annie came through the swinging door. Her cobalt dress made her eyes look more blue than green. With a tub of dirty dishes propped on one hip, she walked two fingers through the air and then flopped her arm to her side.

He laughed and nodded. Her gesture was part of the sign language they'd started developing last night. Her expressive hands said she was exhausted. With this made-up language they could communicate at any time without words, even across a crowded room. Something he'd enjoyed greatly since the diner opened that morning.

But the hunger to talk to her was so strong that he pushed beyond his self-consciousness more than he ever had. Unlike Roman, who had no ability to use his legs, Aden could at least use his voice, and now he had someone worthy of the effort it took to get his ideas across. He'd used every form of communication with her since they'd started work at four that morning—singing, signing, and stuttering.

Mamm walked up to Annie, took the tub of dishes, and set them in the commercial-sized sink. "You've been wonderful help, Annie, but I think I should take you home. We're good here tonight on our own."

Annie's face reflected surprise for a moment. "Oh." She glanced at Aden, hints of embarrassment reflecting in her delicate features.

"Mamm. Don't be r-rude."

"I didn't mean to be." Mamm seemed hurt, but she shook her head.

Annie went to the sink and squirted hot water over the dirty dishes. "I was going to make shoofly pies for tomorrow. It's on the menu, and I mixed the dry ingredients last night for the pie shells and for the crumbs to go in the filling and over the top of the pies."

Mamm seemed perplexed, and guilt nibbled at him. He didn't need to see the fear in her face to know he and Annie were crossing boundaries. The Plain people, Amish or Mennonite, were very clear about those who broke their vow to God concerning the church; it was equal to divorce.

Even Annie's parents weren't divorced. They didn't live together, but they'd never divorce. Mamm opened her mouth to speak but said nothing. The phone rang, and she quickly headed out of the kitchen and toward the cash register, where it sat.

Aden wanted to apologize to Annie and assure her that Mamm was only being protective of them, to tell her they were perfectly safe enjoying each other's company while working…and during the walks they went on after work. But the words jammed inside him, and he didn't even try to stutter his way through. Matching his silence, Annie loaded the plates and cups in the dishwasher.

He put the brush down and wiped his hands on a towel before moving next to her. What he'd give to be able to say a sentence without stammering. He put his hand on her shoulder. "Sh-she's worried."

"I noticed."

Her answer surprised him. "You did?" When she continued working, he put his fingers under the stream of clean water and flicked sprinkles at her.

She barely flinched.

"A-Annie?"

"You and I both know it's forbidden to get close to anyone of the opposite gender from another faith. I don't know about you, but I knelt before God and the church and promised to remain loyal."

"A-a-and?"

She wiped her forehead with her wrist, her hands dripping with water. "That's all I know, Aden." She sounded desperate to drop the topic.

He nudged her with his shoulder and waited for her to look up.

"M-me too." His emotions were everywhere all at once—from friend-ship to obvious sparks of interest. But how could he really know what he felt after only a few days of getting reacquainted?

He and Annie just needed a little time to figure things out.

Or maybe that was the opposite of what they really needed, but it's what he longed for. It's what he'd dreamed of for years, but he'd never dared to cross that line. What did she want?

Mamm walked into the kitchen. "You ready?"

Annie pursed her lips. "Ya."

Aden grabbed the towel off his shoulder and passed it to her.

She dried her hands and gave the towel back. "Bye, Aden."

He wasn't sure what to do, but he knew if she walked out that door right now, nothing between them would be the same. Roman would return next week, and this time with her would be no more than a memory he'd cling to for the rest of his life.

Annie followed his Mamm out of the kitchen. The swinging door swooshed back and forth. Water dripped in the sink. Drip. *Plop.* Drip. *Plop.* The refrigerator hummed. When he was an old man, water would still drip in sinks. Doors would still swoosh. Refrigerators would still run. And he'd still know that he'd let the only woman who ever mattered, ever would matter, walk out of his life. He'd done his best over the years to keep his distance, to live as he'd been taught. He couldn't keep doing that. He just couldn't.

Aden hurried out of the kitchen, but they'd already left. He went outside, caught off guard by the brightness of the day. He blinked and saw them crossing the parking lot. "Annie!"

She turned, said something to his mother, and walked back to him.

He motioned for her to go into the diner, and then he turned to his mother. "W-wait here."

Mamm rubbed her forehead. "Ten minutes."

Aden wouldn't need that long, and if Mamm thought she had the right to dictate his life, she was mistaken.

Annie went inside the diner and leaned against a table, waiting for him to speak.

"M-meet me t-t-tonight?" His question was direct and needed a one-word answer.

But she didn't respond for several moments.

He waited for her reply.

At this rate he'd need a lot longer than ten minutes. Maybe years.

But he understood her hesitation. A positive answer meant they would begin a secret courtship. But how else could they decide what they truly wanted out of this relationship?

"Aden." She fiddled with the buttons on her coat. "I...I want that more than you know, but if my people find out, I'll be set in front of everyone, and if I don't repent, I'll be excommunicated. It's not just me who'll get hurt but my mother and Daadi Moses too. If my mother hasn't already borne enough embarrassment to kill her since Daed walked out, our relationship, if discovered, will surely finish the job. Even your mother wants to put space between us."

He reached into his pants pocket and passed her the folded paper, hoping it said everything he couldn't.

She gasped lightly before she had it fully opened. "Aden." She traced the various hues he'd sketched with the colored pencils.

"You're all I c-can think about."

Her eyes met his. "It's beautiful." She paused, studying it again. "Okay. I'll meet you in the cherry tree orchard tonight."

Nine

*I*rritability snapped throughout Roman like harsh flicks of a whip in the hands of a crazed animal trainer. It was Friday afternoon, and he hadn't spoken to Marian since Wednesday night. He couldn't stand seeing himself as she saw him—too weak to go on a simple date and too uptight to admit it.

Trying not to think about her, he loosened the generator's fan belt. He'd repaired and replaced numerous items on the machine, but its real problem was a broken water pump. He unbolted it from its mount and removed it and the attached fan. He placed them on the table and grabbed the putty knife.

He maneuvered himself as best he could, wishing he could get out of this wheelchair. The more pressure he used to scrape the gasket residue off the mount, the more difficult it became to get positioned right. He set the brake on his wheelchair. Scraped some. Adjusted his chair. Reset the brake. Cleaned another spot. Repositioned his chair. Reset the brake.

Would this be his lot for the rest of his life? Constant tiny shifts and locking into place to accomplish almost nothing?

"Knock, knock." Marian's voice sent a chill up his spine.

"Come on in." He continued his work, hoping he sounded indifferent. There was no way he'd let her know how vulnerable he felt or how disappointed he was in his inability to do something as simple as taking out a girl.

She made no other noise, so he glanced up.

Standing at the far end of the table, she studied him. "Need a hand?"

"Nope." With the mount finally clean, he shifted from the generator to the worktable. He removed the first of four bolts holding the fan.

"Is that the water pump you told me about the other night?" She walked closer.

"Ya."

"It doesn't look broken."

He held it up and pointed at the hairline fracture going through the cast iron.

She frowned. "That little problem brought the whole farm to a halt?"

"Don't be fooled, Marian." He sounded as unyielding as the iron in his hand, and he wondered if it bothered her. "A tiny fracture can ruin the strongest thing on this planet—be it an element of nature, man-made, or man himself."

She removed the new water pump from its opened box and turned it one way and then the other, studying it.

"Be careful with that." He removed the last of the four bolts and separated the fan from the water pump. "It may be the last of its kind."

"It doesn't look new."

"It's not. But it's solid."

Once they'd figured out the problem, Ernie's Englischer mechanic had spent a full day searching the Internet and making calls to find a replacement water pump. After he'd found one, he had FedEx overnight it, and it'd been delivered this morning. Even though it wasn't new, it was sound and should last for years, giving Ernie time to save enough money to replace the generator.

She set it on the table. "Things ended on an awkward note the other night."

"I know. I was there."

"But for the life of me, I can't figure out what went wrong."

Roman scoffed. "It all started when you insisted I come to your place to pick you up."

"That's how dates work."

Roman faced her squarely. "Look at me, Marian. I don't *work* normal."

"Then you should have said so," she snapped. "You balked at coming to get me, and I asked if there was a problem. If you had answered honestly, we would've made other plans."

"It doesn't matter now." He wheeled himself to the far end of the table and picked up the small can of High Tack. "We had an awful time, and you get to blame me. Are you done with your pity dates for the year, or do I have to go through that one more time just to prove that you don't have the heart for cripple dating?"

"You know, Roman,"—she grabbed the arm of his wheelchair and turned him to face her—"I had a pretty nice time, but I really appreciate knowing you didn't."

Roman set the can in his lap and leaned away from her. She'd had a nice time? He had, but he'd assumed…

She released his chair. "The problem isn't that you were dishonest with me or that you're in a wheelchair."

He didn't know where she was heading with her argument, and he didn't want to know. Whether she admitted it today or next month, he knew they had no future. "I'm glad you have me all figured out, Marian, but I've got too much to do and no time for your opinion on my problems."

He went around her and returned to the generator. He opened the small can and used the attached brush to apply the sealant between the gasket and the mounting surface.

"Roman." Marian sounded dismayed. "Is that it? One date that didn't work out and you're giving up?"

"You can't tell me what I should do, think, or feel. You're not the one sitting in this chair, needing someone to help get you up in the morning or in and out of rigs or into homes because steps block the way."

He grabbed the cast-iron water pump by the shaft. It rotated, pinching his fingers, and he jerked his hand away. The pump fell onto his knee before it crashed to the floor.

Marian rushed to his side. "Are you hurt?"

The water pump lay on the concrete floor, a few mounting pieces scattered. Nausea roiled, and he feared he was about to throw up on her. He bent, reaching as far as he could, trying to grab it.

Marian picked it up and handed it to him. A jagged line ran the length of it, and his heart sank. He brushed his fingers over the fracture. "It's ruined."

Marian jerked straight pins from her apron and took it off. She folded it and held it out to him. "Put this on your leg and press down."

He looked where the ten-pound iron pump had banged into his knee and saw blood seeping through his pants. He had diminished feeling in his thighs, but his emotional turmoil was what had kept him from noticing it until now. Instead of taking the apron, he backed away from her. "Just leave. Please."

"No. We need to go inside and get your leg cleaned up and bandaged."

"Marian, this is a disaster. My uncle is counting on me, and that pump was his only hope."

She put her apron back on, avoiding eye contact with him. "If that man found one pump, I'm sure he can find another. But right now, that's not the problem. Your leg is."

"Marian, look at me!"

When she did, he saw more strength in her than in himself.

He clutched the hand rims of his wheelchair. "I'm not joking around." He moved himself a little closer, trying to look assertive. "Go away."

She peered down at him, looking both sincere and angry. "Now I understand why you didn't have enough to say to keep on writing. You're not the same Roman I knew."

He scoffed. "You just figured that out? You must've graduated at the top of your class."

She started to leave, then turned to him. "If you ever grow up and let go of self-pity, let me know."

He held up his hand. "Just go, Marian. Nothing about me will ever change for the better."

She stared at him for a moment before leaving and closing the door behind her.

He looked at his bleeding leg. As soon as Marian left the farm, he'd go inside and tend to it.

The broken water pump in his hand mocked him. Ernie had trusted him to fix the generator, and all he'd managed to do was make things worse. How was he going to tell his uncle?

***

The wooden stairs creaked mercilessly as Annie tiptoed down them in the dark. Once at the bottom, she crept slowly toward the back door. The old farmhouse moaned with every move she made, as if she weighed hundreds of pounds. And with guilt strapped to her back, she felt as heavy as an elephant.

She turned the old black doorknob. Daadi once said that the brass had been shiny in its day. But now the doorknob was discolored and wobbly, and the skeleton key had long ago been lost, so the door was always unlocked.

Stepping onto the back porch, she eased the door shut. Once

across the back porch, she hurried down the steps. The night air seemed even warmer this evening. Stars shone brightly overhead, and in the distance she could see the silhouette of branches against the foggy sky.

As she walked toward the orchard, her guilt gave way to excitement. After Aden had given her the picture earlier today, she wanted to see him more than she'd ever wanted anything. Wrong as it might be, she could not be controlled by the remorse she had for her actions. They were both believers in God's Word. How wrong could they be to fall in love?

In the distance she spotted Aden's rig parked in the same place as before. She scanned the orchard and thought she saw movement in the fog near the creek bed. Heading that way, her heart pounded like crazy. It wasn't like her to do anything behind people's backs. She had always been open and honest…well she had with her outward actions, but she'd also carried a smoldering flame for Aden for quite a while.

"Hello, Annie." Aden was singing an unfamiliar tune. "I thought maybe you'd changed your mind."

She spun around. "Where are you?"

He stepped out of the mist, causing a swirl of fog around him. "Here." He motioned for her. "I want to show you something."

She walked beside him, wondering the name of the song he was using to fill with his own words. It seemed both haunting and feathery light.

Once near the creek, they stepped onto a large rock. "I can hardly see anything."

"Make sure your feet are planted firmly, and we won't move from here until time to leave." He towered over her, his body mere inches away, emanating kindness and patience.

"Aden?" She wanted to know what they were doing, but they both knew. They were breaking the rules and falling in love.

"What is it, my friend?" He sang, using a tune that gave his words an unusual, rhythmic cadence.

She wouldn't ask him questions about things neither of them was ready to talk about. "I don't know that tune. Where did you hear it?"

"Mamm taught it to me years ago. She said that when she was a little girl, she went with her mother to clean houses for an Englischer woman, and the woman always had a John Denver record playing. Mamm sang one of the songs to Roman and me over and over when we were little. I'd forgotten about it until you returned. It's called 'Annie's Song.' "

"There's a song with my name in it?"

"I don't think the lyrics have your name. Just the title."

"I like the tune."

"The music fits you, Annie." His whisper entered her, changing her somehow.

"Sing it for me."

He stood on the rock, singing softly, painting beautiful images about mountains and springtime, a walk in the rain, and a storm in the desert. He hummed a few lines, and she thought maybe he'd forgotten the lyrics, but then he sang a line about giving his life to her, drowning in her laughter, wanting to die in her arms. When he stopped, she longed to hear it again. But words failed her, and she stood in silence.

The real world seemed distant. Even the cherry tree orchard didn't look the same as she and Aden stood side by side. Guilt nibbled, but she longed for a thousand nights with Aden. Tens of thousands, really.

And it scared her. "Aden, what are we doing?"

"Look around you, Annie." He spoke softly, without stumbling over his words. "We're in a fog. But we're together. That's all I need."

Calmness poured over her.

Was this love? Connecting with someone in a way that was impossible with all others? If so, she was glad she hadn't let Mamm pressure her into settling for Leon. How awful to think about, now that she'd experienced the thrill of a heart-pounding bond. She willed herself not to care who approved or disapproved of their seeing each other.

He made no effort even to hold her hand. She trusted that he was respecting the ways of her people and their policy of hands-off dating only. That teaching was as old as the Mennonite faith itself. In the strictest sense, the church taught that couples weren't even to hold hands until they were wed. But the Amish allowed rumschpringe.

"How many girls have you courted?"

He shrugged, clearly not wanting to talk about it.

"I've dated before." She shuddered. "Mostly it was awful. Ever been on a terrible date when you couldn't wait until it was over?"

"N-no."

"You're lucky. That's all I've ever had until this week. When I joined the church at seventeen, I was so excited at the prospect of dating. I've only dated one guy, but I quickly decided that a dead fish has more personality than we did together."

He chuckled.

"Mamm was disappointed when I stopped seeing him." Annie shuddered at the thought of Mamm discovering her interest in Aden.

Her family would be just as upset with her seeing someone Amish as they would be if she decided to leave the church and chase after the world. When she thought about the seriousness of the vow she'd taken, she understood how they could feel that strongly. Even so, caring for Aden couldn't be compared to pursuing lusts. But folks would see it in the same light, and the Mennonites were as firm in their beliefs as the Amish were in theirs.

Worse, thunder would shake the ground for years to come if Daadi Moses found out. And if she didn't end it with Aden immediately, Daadi, the church, and the entire Mennonite community would disown her.

Her good mood threatened to disperse like fog under the morning sunlight. She tugged on Aden's coat sleeve and then got off the rock and moved away from the creek. "I should get back."

Walking side by side, they meandered through the orchard until her grandfather's house came into sight. "You should go now."

He kept walking beside her. "M-meet me in the orchard tomorrow night?"

As he studied her, she knew she'd not refuse him. "Okay. Good night, Aden." She turned to go toward the house and glanced at her Daadi's bedroom window. Certain she saw curtains shift, fear rippled through her.

Ten

*E*llen wished she was pounding a batch of bread dough as her brother explained over the phone what had happened to Roman.

Her son had failed. The gash in his leg would heal, not as quickly as it would for someone with mobility, but with proper care it wouldn't become a problem. What she couldn't do anything about was his inability to fix the generator. She'd sent him to Ernie's, positive he'd return with dignity and excitement at what he could accomplish. Instead, a driver would pull up in the driveway within the hour, and Roman would arrive home defeated.

Ernie apologized and told her they'd done all they could to assure Roman it wasn't his fault and it wasn't a big deal.

But it was. And everyone knew it.

"My Englischer friend couldn't find another water pump, so I'll go to the bank on Monday and begin the process of trying to secure a loan." Her brother tried to sound upbeat.

"You could ask the community to help."

"You know the collective fund is for emergencies, when a family has no other options. I'm not there…yet."

Ellen said good-bye and hung up. Weariness wrapped around her shoulders as she left the phone shanty. She stood beside her barren garden, praying for strength.

"Mamm?" Arie called. "I have soup and sandwiches ready. Daed helped me some."

Her ten-year-old daughter sounded pleased with her accomplishment. Arie's older sister usually made lunch for the family on Saturdays, but Mary was at the restaurant today, helping Aden. "Coming."

The moment Ellen walked in and her husband caught a glimpse of her, concern lined his face.

"Mamm, look." Arie stood at the head of a perfectly set table. "I did it by myself."

"Very nice, dear. Denki."

David came to her. "Ellen, what's wrong?" Her husband's whisper gave her strength.

"Roman dropped the replacement water pump, and it broke. He's on his way home. As soon as the children are finished eating, one of us needs to take them to the diner so the other can have a bit of time alone with Roman."

"I think he's most likely to hear you." He kissed her cheek. "We'll get him through this. You know we will."

She nodded, more to assure him than anything. Her mother heart broke for her son.

Lunch passed smoothly, then she helped David hitch a horse to a carriage and get their four youngest children seated inside the rig.

They'd barely pulled onto the road when a driver arrived with

Roman. She hurried to the passenger door and opened it. When his eyes met hers, she saw the rawness of his pain.

Mamm kissed his cheek. "I'm so glad you're home. We missed you."

"Denki, Mamm." His voice carried so much gloom it didn't even sound familiar.

She stepped back as the driver handed her Roman's traveling bag and then lifted him into the wheelchair. Roman paid him, saying thanks. Mamm set the bag on the sidewalk and faced him.

She stared into his eyes, feeling tears well. "I'm sorry, Roman."

For a brief moment she saw a man too broken to respond. His eyes misted. "Me too."

She studied him, looking for signs of hope or strength to build on, but she saw none.

"What are you doing, Mamm, praying for a miracle that'll get me out of this wheelchair?"

During the first few weeks after the accident, she'd prayed night and day for divine healing for both her son and her husband. "No. You are already a miracle. You survived, and you've helped this family survive."

He lowered his eyes, tears falling. She knew he wasn't convinced that his being alive was a gift to anyone, most of all to himself.

"Kumm." Mamm moved behind him, took hold of the hand-grips, and pushed him up the ramp and into the house. The place smelled of freshly perked coffee and pie, both of which she'd begun preparing after Ernie had called. She released his chair and took off her sweater. "Are you hungry?"

He shook his head and wheeled farther into the house. She went to the stove and poured him a cup of coffee.

When she set the steamy mug at his place on the kitchen table, he moved into the one spot that hadn't held a chair in five years. She removed the ground cherry pie from the oven, cut two slices, and set them on the table. After passing him a fork and napkin, she took a seat.

He sipped the coffee a time or two as the minutes ticked by. "I can't stop wishing things…wishing *I* was different." He stared at the black liquid in his cup. "Daed hobbles through his days. Aden stutters, when he talks at all. And I'm in this contraption." He fidgeted with the mug, looking lost inside himself. "I guess God doesn't do miracles for people like us."

It was the first time in years he'd mentioned his disappointment in God saving his life but not the use of his legs. She reached across the table and covered his hand with hers. "Roman, my prayer for you isn't for a miraculous healing of your spinal cord. It's for you to be healed of blindness so you can see your life through faith."

He picked up a fork and poked at the dessert. "Ya, whatever." After several long minutes, he put down his fork. "Tell me the truth, Mamm. Doesn't it bother you that we look like a bunch of cursed idiots to everyone around us?"

"The absolute truth?"

"Ya."

"Not one iota. Some families are handsome and look perfect. Some are wealthy. Some are particularly smart. Some are homely. Poor. Not too bright. And some struggle no matter how hard they try. But we all have one thing in common—not one person or family is worth anything unless they're walking by faith."

"Faith." He said it as if it were a foreign word he was trying to understand. "Belief in what we can't see." He mumbled the words, sounding confused.

"The passage that says faith believes in what it can't see means much more than believing in an invisible God. It also includes having faith in the things about yourself and your life that are hidden from view."

He lifted his fork and took a bite of pie. "Maybe."

Ellen prayed silently, asking God to plant seeds in her son's heart and water them. If Roman could see his life through the eyes of faith, he'd find his way.

A loud rap at the back door startled her. She got up. "Sounds like we have visitors on a Saturday afternoon. Maybe it'll be someone willing to eat that pie you're turning your nose up at."

When she opened the door, she was mildly surprised to see Moses. He didn't come over often, usually to see if they needed anything when he'd heard that David was having a bad spell. But David wasn't down, and concern ran through her. "Good afternoon. Would you care to come in?"

He shook his head. "What I have to say needs to be said in private." Moses's voice was so soft she'd barely heard him. "Do you prefer I talk to David or you?"

Moses was a peculiar man, and she'd yet to figure him out. She stepped onto the porch, closing the door behind her. "He and the children are at the diner for the afternoon. What seems to be the matter?"

"Your father-in-law and I went into business together years before your husband was born. And even though he's been gone a long time, I've tried to be a good partner to your husband and sons and a good neighbor."

"And you've succeeded on every count."

He removed his hat. "I don't want to do anybody different than I want to be done by God. I'm getting old, and my time's drawing closer to standing before Him and giving an answer for how I've lived. I'm gonna ask for mercy, and that means I gotta give it. But I also got to protect what's mine, Ellen."

Her mouth went dry. "Have we done something wrong?"

"I woke during the night and found that my granddaughter was gone. While watching for her to return, I saw your son walking her home from the orchard. I want all contact with her stopped. Immediately."

"What? But I thought…" Yesterday Ellen had made it clear to Aden that he and Annie had to put distance between themselves. After Annie had spoken privately with Aden while Ellen waited in the carriage, Annie returned visibly shaken. Ellen had foolishly assumed—or maybe just hoped—that they'd settled matters between them. Annie hadn't returned to the restaurant since then, but clearly things were not over. "I…I didn't know. I'll speak to him."

"It'll take more than speaking to him. You and David have to put your foot down. Aden has to be made to understand—"

Ellen leaned in. "Just Aden? Was Annie not also in that orchard?"

Moses suddenly looked much like a deflated balloon. "I insisted her mother marry, and we all know how that turned out. Will I now have to be the one to insist my granddaughter not see someone she obviously cares about?" He rubbed his forehead. "Her mother can't even tolerate talking to me on the phone. Annie is all I've got, and I don't want to turn her against me, but I won't have her reputation dragged through the mud like her mother's was."

Ellen wanted to assure him that Annie would never be so foolish as to allow her reputation to be ruined, but the words stuck in her throat. If word of her and Aden's late night stroll got out, the damage would be unstoppable.

Moses nervously fiddled with his hat and stared at the floor. "If I have to intervene to keep them apart, I will." He raised his eyes, looking torn between determination and grief. "But if I do step in, I'll do *whatever* it takes to keep them apart."

Fear and offense twisted her insides, battling so strong she could hardly speak. "What are you saying, Moses?"

"You remind Aden of the connection I've had with this family for three generations, of all I did during the tragedy you faced five years ago. Then you tell him that no upstanding Mennonite will take a second glance at a girl who once saw an Amish man behind everyone's back. Make him see this for what it is, Ellen."

Tears welled, and she cleared her throat. "I'll try."

He started down the steps. Then he stopped and turned back. "I…I've got to tell you the rest." He shifted. "I'm sorry for what I'm about to say. I am, but I've got to do what's best for everyone, Annie most of all. If Aden refuses to listen despite your warnings, I'll move, taking Annie with me so she can have a fresh start."

"Moses, your land and your life are here."

"Nothing is more important to me than Annie. Will I stay here because this is home and thereby allow my granddaughter to break her vow to God? Is your son not in the same position before the Almighty? If they break this vow, will they not easily break more vows as they go through life and then be in jeopardy of the gates of hell?"

He'd finally spoken his biggest fear—that Aden and Annie's relationship would destroy the one between each of them and God. The church taught that a vow before God should never be broken. Maybe that was too strict. Maybe it wasn't. Ellen had no way of knowing for sure, not this side of heaven. She'd been a fool not to see the full weight of things before now.

Moses put on his hat, but his shoulders remained slumped. "If I need to go so far as to leave Apple Ridge, I'll close out my businesses."

As veiled as his threat was, she heard him clearly. If Aden continued seeing his granddaughter, he'd leave with her, pulling his partnership from the restaurant in the process. Without a Mennonite as a business partner, they'd lose their right to have electricity supplied to the diner, and they'd have to shut the place down immediately, or the state would do it for them. If Aden continued seeing a Mennonite girl, no other Mennonite would ever partner with them.

Moses closed his eyes, shaking all over. "I don't want to be this way. Surely you know that. But I will protect Annie at any cost."

The back door opened, interrupting her thoughts. "Moses." Roman glanced at Mamm. "It's good to see you. Would you care to come inside?"

Moses shook his head, but Ellen knew what her son was doing. Roman had seen them through the window, maybe heard one or two things, and he'd come out to check on her.

"Ellen. Roman." Moses nodded curtly to each of them. "Good day."

Once back in the kitchen, Roman whirled his wheelchair around and glared up at his mother. "What was that about?"

"Nothing I want to talk about."

"I heard him say Annie's name. What's going on?"

Ellen sat at the table and held her head with one hand. "Annie helped out at the diner while you were gone, and…it seems she and Aden took a liking to each other. I've been hoping it'd blow over, even thought they'd agreed not to see each other anymore. But it seems I was wrong."

"I thought the family was going to help at the diner while I was gone."

"We did." She took the pie plates and forks off the table and headed to the sink. Her son was certainly not going to eat his slice now. "But Annie showed up to visit her Daadi, and she came over to be of some assistance to me. I invited her to help us—"

A loud crash made her jerk around. Shards of Roman's cup were spread all over the counter and the floor. Splashes of coffee trickled down the walls. Ellen put the plates and forks on the counter.

She'd watched Roman struggle with frustration over his circumstances—he'd had a tempest brewing in his soul for five years. But she hadn't expected it to be unleashed on her kitchen wall.

Ellen went to the walk-in pantry and grabbed a broom and a long-handled dustpan. "I think I have more than enough on me right now without you adding to it. So you clean it up, and don't forget to wipe the walls down with a clean, wet rag." She didn't know how great a job he could do from his chair, but she wasn't doing it for him.

Roman's face was carved with anger, but he took the items from her and swept broken glass into the pan. "We can't afford to make Moses angry. He could ruin everything for us."

"Ya, he said as much just now."

Roman gritted his teeth. "Aden can't endanger the family's livelihood over a girl. What is he thinking?"

Ellen understood Aden's pull toward Annie. She had inner strength and was deeply kind. She had a wonderful sense of humor and was very industrious. Moreover, she drew out the very best of Aden. If she were Amish, she'd be the answer to Ellen's prayers. In fact, she'd hoped Annie's friendship with the Zooks would continue forever, even after Aden married and had a family of his own. Now that dream was shattered just like Roman's mug. Broken beyond repair.

Roman continued maneuvering shards into the dustpan. "When I was at Uncle Ernie's, working on that generator, I started to get back that feeling I used to have whenever I did something mechanical with my hands. I really believed I could fix that thing. Even thought maybe I could start doing machine repair for a living…if the family could manage the diner without me."

His jaw tightened. "But I made matters worse for Ernie." He turned to her. "And Aden was here, making things worse for this family. I was beating myself up over my incident, and it was an accident. There is no excuse for what Aden's doing."

Ellen laid a hand on her son's stiff shoulder. "I'll talk to him. It's all we can do."

"Oh, that may be all you're willing to do. But if he doesn't listen, I'll do more than just talk."

"Like what?" she challenged him, sounding cynical.

"I'm not sure, but I know we can't let this situation with Aden and Annie continue." Roman went to the window and studied the outside as if longing to step into a different world.

"You stay out of this, Roman. No sneaky, manipulative tricks. That will only make matters worse. He's your brother. Pray for him. Be patient. And don't do anything stupid."

Eleven

*A*den sat at a table filled with people in Mattie's parents' home. The wedding ceremony was over, and the celebrations had begun. Guests chatted and joked throughout the big, formal meal of the day. Aden tried to stomach enough food so he didn't draw attention to himself, but he didn't really hear anything that was said.

When the mealtime was over, he took his glass of water with him as he searched for a place to hide. His mother had confronted him about Annie on Saturday night. Today was Tuesday, and her words continued to loop through his mind. But it was the depth of hurt and concern in her eyes and the trembling of her hands that haunted him the most—that and the threat that now hovered over his family. His whole family would pay, would be thrown into a poverty pit, if he and Annie didn't go their separate ways.

He went to a quiet spot and stared out a window, wondering what Annie was doing today. He'd still gone to the orchard every night since Mamm had informed him of the ultimatum Moses had issued, but he hadn't told Annie about it yet. He'd tried to talk about the seriousness of what they were doing. His plan was to ease into the fact that her grandfather knew and had hung a threat over his family. But she cut him off before he explained anything, saying she didn't want to talk about it. Truth was, neither did he. Did raising the stakes really matter? They both knew what they were doing was wrong in the eyes of their churches. Maybe in the eyes of God.

Even if Mattie and Gideon could've invited her to the wedding, Aden wouldn't have been able to do more than speak to her for a few minutes. Less than three or four, really. Anything more would have caused a ripple of people questioning their friendship.

They wouldn't be the only ones. He had lots of questions himself. Why was this happening to them? How was he ever going to return to his usual life once she was gone? Her presence filled his life, and her absence would leave an awful void. Could they hang on to each other and muddle through everyone's disapproval? Or would he ruin her life and his family's livelihood by trying to find a way for them to be together?

If she had come today, she'd have felt the weight of being an outsider. Even though she had a passing acquaintance with Mattie's and Gideon's out-of-town wedding guests who'd come into the diner last week, she hardly knew any of the local Amish. Aden had attended church meetings and Amish gatherings his whole life, so he knew almost everyone…except a few of Mattie's Amish friends from Ohio who had arrived last night.

Out in the yard a small group of girls about Annie's age talked and laughed. The guests were milling about inside and outside while the helpers cleaned up after the noon meal. Soon the single girls would disappear into a room to prepare for the Amish tradition of the Choosing, where men chose partners for the wedding festivities of singing, passing around snacks, playing a few games, and sharing the evening meal. Custom called for the unmarried men, from eldest to youngest, to enter the room one at a time to make their choices.

If Annie were here, she wouldn't be allowed to participate in the Amish Choosing. If there were a few single Mennonites here, they'd have their own Choosing. Otherwise, she'd be left out completely.

Throughout the ceremony Aden couldn't keep from imagining himself and Annie in place of Gideon and Mattie. How had his friendship with Annie so quickly grown into desire for a lifetime with her?

An Amish girl bounded in through the door, flashing a quick smile at everyone before continuing into the living room. There were several single men here older than Aden, and he speculated what girls might be left by the time his turn came at the Choosing. He'd like it if no one was still available, but there were a lot of girls at this wedding. Most young women made their preferences clear by either looking up or glancing away when a man came into the room. Aden hoped to avoid the embarrassment of choosing from a group of girls who all looked away when he entered.

Annie saw past his inability to speak smoothly. She always had. And he believed in himself. He hoped that wasn't prideful, but despite how others saw him, he sensed his value—he had a lot to offer if given the chance. It was there inside him, like a pouch of silver hidden in a rocky field, just waiting for the owner to need it enough to dig it out of the packed earth.

Even Roman, who knew him better than anyone, seemed to see Aden as less worthy. Maybe he always had. And until recently, Aden had accepted and tolerated his brother's opinion.

He shifted, wishing he could sigh without being noticed. Several young women came in the front door and giggled as they made their way to the Choosing room. Though the coupling was only for the day, Aden had no desire to pretend to be interested in any of them.

A wedding partner didn't need to do much. Just keep the chosen girl company throughout the day's activities. If friends planned a wedding prank that required masculine assistance, he usually got roped into that as well. Aden didn't mind helping with wedding pranks, all harmless fun. Last year some guests barricaded the bride and her friends in her parents' home. The grin on the bride's face when she finally escaped from the house and flew into her new husband's arms was priceless.

"Aden." The floorboards creaked under Roman's wheelchair as he entered the room. "What are you doing standing off in a corner?"

He turned to face his brother. "H-hiding."

He chuckled. "And hoping there won't be any girls left when your turn comes?"

Aden returned his attention to the window. His brother knew him well.

Roman wheeled up beside him. "See that girl in the blue dress?" He pointed to a large oak in the yard where a petite brunette stood in the shade of the tree trunk, talking to a taller, slender blond.

Aden nodded.

"I want to choose her."

Aden raised an eyebrow and shrugged, silently asking his brother why he wasn't out there talking to her right now.

Roman stared at his legs. "I can't take her anywhere by myself." He looked up, a hint of hope in his eyes. "But if you chose her friend, we could all be together."

"N-no way." Aden peered at the petite girl's friend. He couldn't see her very well from this distance, especially in the shadow of the tree. But her appearance made no difference. She could be a troll, and she'd still be better off with anyone other than him. Stuttering aside, it wasn't right to spend the day with a girl and be thinking about someone else the whole time.

"We can work together like we do at the diner. I'll help you communicate, and you can help me get around. Come on, what do you say?"

Aden looked into Roman's pleading eyes.

Mattie's Daed clapped his hands. "Time for the Choosing."

"Please," Roman whispered.

Worse yet, if he agreed to this arrangement, it meant the four of them would take a carriage ride after the day's events, like a double date. And that would keep them out past ten—the time he'd agreed to meet Annie at the orchard.

But his brother needed this. Desperately. Aden prayed Annie would understand why he couldn't meet her tonight.

"Okay. I'll do it."

Annie flung dried corn onto the ground as chickens clucked all around her, pecking in the loose dirt. This small brood was her grandfather's personal laying hens. All she wanted was to get done with her chores and find a way to check on Aden. He'd never showed last night, and her fears for his safety were mounting by the minute. Rarely did a week pass without her reading about a horse-and-carriage wreck in the newspaper. She hadn't slept all night and had grabbed the paper first thing. Nothing was listed.

Daadi Moses was somewhere on the egg farm, probably working harder than most men half his age, but lately he hadn't wanted her help with those jobs, so she'd been keeping her distance. This morning he'd do well to stay out of her way. Despite her best efforts, she was much like a wet hen, ruffling her feathers every few minutes and slinging dirty water in every direction.

While waiting last night for Aden, she'd walked up from the creek to the top of the knoll dozens of times, looking for signs of him. She'd then returned to the orchard, thinking maybe he'd decided to walk from his place rather than come by carriage. She'd diligently watched for him, determined not to miss him no matter what part of the acreage he might be on. But he'd never showed.

She emptied the pan of chicken feed. After turning on the spigot, she filled the containers with fresh water, trying to calm her rioting emotions. She had to see him this morning, and she intended to be there the minute the diner opened.

After turning off the water and closing the gate to the chicken pen, she hurried into the farmhouse to wash up. Daadi Moses had told her she couldn't use the rig to go to the diner anymore, so she'd go on foot. That was not what he'd intended when he said she couldn't drive over there, but she had to check on Aden this morning.

The mid-March sun was warm on her back. The newspaper said the high today would be sixty with a light wind. But by the time she stood across the street from the diner a couple of miles from her grandfather's place, she was ready to pull off her jacket.

She stared at the diner from the far side of the street. Through the large plate-glass window, it appeared that Aden was in the kitchen. Relief lasted only a moment before insecurity reared its head. Perhaps he'd changed his mind about her.

They'd had five glorious late-night strolls, talking about anything and everything. Reminiscing about childhood memories. Sharing their opinions about the differing views of their communities. Discussing their hopes and dreams for the future. Of course, Annie had done most of the talking. But Aden had started to come out of his protective shell.

She loved the way he sang his more intimate thoughts to her. But she rejoiced especially when he was able to speak without singing or stuttering, at least not as much as before.

The night before last, they'd stayed together the latest, neither of them wanting their time together to end. That's how she'd felt, at least. She'd assumed he thought the same thing.

But if he felt the way she did, then why did he stand her up last night?

The question circled, making her heart ache.

Roman came to the front door and flipped the Closed sign to Open. A family of eight piled out of a car in the parking lot and entered the restaurant. Roman welcomed them in and showed them to a table. His smiling face indicated that all was well.

Needing answers, she strode across the street and opened the glass door. When Roman turned her way, she smiled. His expression turned cold.

He grabbed a menu and rolled toward her. "Table for one?"

This was not one of the countless scenarios she'd envisioned. He'd asked that as if she were a customer he didn't like.

"I'm here to see Aden." Her voice sounded weak.

"He's busy."

She looked toward the pass-through, but Aden was no longer in sight. The family she'd seen walk in were the only people in the diner. "Well, if you're going to be busy today, maybe I can help again."

"Annie," Roman whispered, "be reasonable, please. We can't afford to anger Moses. You know that." He gestured at the customer tables. "But you're welcome to eat here anytime. Would you prefer a table or a booth?"

Was Roman speaking for Aden, telling her it was over? She wouldn't know unless she spoke to him. "No thanks. I'll just sit at the counter." She walked past him and perched on the stool with the best view of the kitchen. It looked as it always did first thing in the morning—except she didn't see or hear any sign of Aden.

Ellen came out of the dry pantry with a large can of pepper. She grabbed a pitcher of water from a serving station and walked up to the occupied table. "Good morning." She refilled their glasses. "Did Roman get your order already?" They nodded. "I'll have your food ready in a jiffy."

She headed for the kitchen but stopped short. "Annie, I...I didn't know you were here." Her eyes reflected something far different from the welcome she'd received little more than a week ago. "Can I make you something for breakfast?"

What was going on with this family?

"Is Aden here?"

Ellen bit her lower lip. "He's in the deep freeze, taking inventory, while we handle the diner. He used up a lot of supplies last week, and we have to get a careful accounting so we can get our order in this afternoon." She hustled into the kitchen as if Annie had a contagious disease.

Her heart aching, Annie had to own up to what was going on. They knew about her and Aden, and the frosty responses would be commonplace from now on. Still, she had to speak to Aden. Would he treat her with cold politeness too?

She went into the kitchen and straight to the freezer, ignoring Ellen. The heavy stainless steel door was propped open slightly by a cinder block. She grabbed the handle and pulled. Aden had on his coat and was taking notes on a clipboard. She stepped inside and allowed the door to slowly close until it bumped the block.

When his eyes met hers, he seemed both glad and startled. "A-Annie," he whispered, "what are you d-doing here?"

She wrapped her arms around herself. "I was concerned about you."

Aden took off his coat and put it around her shoulders. "I c-couldn't make it."

"What happened?"

He shifted, looking uncomfortable. "I…I…"

"Aden, where's the…" Roman jerked open the door. "Oh, Annie." He wheeled over the rubberized lip and came inside. "I thought you'd left."

She looked to Aden, unable to read his thoughts.

Roman shook his head disapprovingly and started to leave, and then he stopped. "Don't stay too long, Annie. We have work to catch up on after last week's busyness and closing yesterday for the wedding. After last night, Aden's moving as slowly today as me. But it was worth it, wasn't it, brother?"

"Shut up," Aden growled without stuttering.

Annie's fingertips tingled with numbness. "What do you mean?"

"Aden may not be ready to tell you, so maybe I should just go."

"Finish what you started, Roman," Annie demanded.

"It's just that we had a late night out with a couple of lovely women." Roman lifted his chin, seeming very pleased. "We took them for a buggy ride after the wedding guests left the bride and groom for the evening. My girl kept staring at my worthless legs, but Aden's partner sure took a liking to him."

"R-Roman!" Aden pointed at the door, inviting him to leave.

He winked. "I think he's embarrassed to talk about how well things went for him."

Annie studied Aden, feeling sick. He hadn't wanted her to know…but it was time to face the truth. Any Amish girl would be a better fit for him than her. "If you'll excuse me, I need to go home." She removed his coat, and when he didn't take it, she dropped it and hurried out of there as fast as her unsteady legs would move.

Twelve

*E*llen went to the front porch and rang the dinner bell, knowing it'd take her family a few minutes to come from wherever they were. She waited and then rang it again before returning to the kitchen. After grabbing a set of potholders, she opened the oven. The biscuits were a golden brown.

A loud slamming noise echoed through the house, and she nearly dropped the pan of biscuits. It wasn't a door that had been knocked shut. Maybe the lid to Aden's footlocker.

"Dinner," she called out.

The four younger children scampered in from their chores, chattering about how hungry they were as they washed up in the mud sink near the back door.

The noise seemed to have come from her sons' room, so she headed that way. Ever since Annie had left the diner this morning, Aden had been furious with his brother. Her stomach had knotted when she saw Annie flee the restaurant. Such a sweet girl. Did she know her presence could lead them into poverty?

As she walked toward their room, David came in from the field. After talking to Aden about Moses's visit, she'd told David what was going on. He'd chosen to stay out of it for now, not wanting Aden to feel they were ganging up on him. Ellen tapped on her sons' door. She heard nothing, so she knocked again.

Roman jerked open the door and wheeled out of the bedroom, looking angrier than she'd ever seen him. Aden sat on his bed, refusing even to glance her way. The situation between Aden and Annie was a grave one, but Ellen wondered if part of Roman's real problem was that his twin brother had been doing something he hadn't shared with him.

"Dinner," she repeated. No matter what stress their family went through, they'd always found peace and unity while sharing a meal. He got up and went to the table, but a current of tension came into the room with him.

During their moment of silent prayer before the meal, Ellen opened her eyes just long enough to notice that her twin sons sat stone faced.

David helped himself to a large spoonful of mashed potatoes, then passed the bowl to Roman. "Either of you boys care to talk about what's going on between you?"

Roman cast a threatening glance at his brother, who shot back a look of warning. "Aden has violated the church rules, Daed. Not once, but repeatedly."

Aden snatched the serving bowl from Roman. The other children's eyes darted from their older brothers to their father.

"Recently?" David asked.

Aden smacked a spoonful of potatoes onto his plate before passing it. "Ya."

"He's been sneaking out at night to see Annie," Roman blurted.

Aden pointed at his brother. "And you're a bald-faced liar. You think my seeing Annie is worse than your looking her in the eyes and lying to her?" Aden's stuttering all but disappeared when he got extremely angry—a rare occurrence.

Ellen's throat tightened as she passed the green beans.

David ignored his plate of hot food and stared at Aden. "What do you have to say for yourself, Son?"

"I have nothing to be ashamed of."

"Then why were you trying to keep it a secret?" Roman asked.

"Why did you lie to her about the girl at the wedding?"

"That's enough, both of you." David hacked at his slice of beef as if he were sawing a hickory limb. "I can't believe you would do this to the man who saved our family from ruin." Instead of eating the bite he'd cut, he started ripping at another one. "If Moses hadn't poured his time and energy into that diner after the accident, we would have lost our ability to keep food on this table." Having cut his entire slice of beef into small bites, he finally put one in his mouth.

"And I'm g-g-grateful for e-everything he—"

David shook his head. "If you were so grateful, you wouldn't betray him by trying to steal his granddaughter."

"I didn't st-steal anything. I just—"

"Annie means everything to Moses." David put his fork and knife down. "He sees her as the only good fruit his life has borne. Even if you could convince her to give up everything for you, Moses would never allow it. He certainly wouldn't continue partnering with us on the diner, and without the electricity he provides, the state will shut the place down. How could you risk your family's livelihood over something that cannot possibly work out, no matter how much you want it to?"

Ellen's heart wept for Aden. But she wanted to smack Roman for the smug expression on his face. She wouldn't, but she wanted to.

"What about all the hard work I've put into the diner—and this family?" Aden's ire was up again, and he didn't stutter one word. "Do I complain? No, I just keep going. Carrying him, and he treats me like a slave and then ruins the only good thing I have."

Although Aden didn't look at Roman when he said it, his brother's shoulders drooped. Ellen was shocked at her typically reserved son's outburst, but maybe this is what Roman needed to hear.

David unclenched his teeth. "From now on, you will leave that girl alone. You are never to see her again. Is that understood?"

Aden tossed his cloth napkin over the barely touched food on his plate. "I don't need your permission or Roman's to do anything." He stood and walked out of the house.

Ellen stared after her son, unwilling to turn and see the anguish she knew she'd find on the faces of her husband, Roman, and even her younger children.

She hoped Aden would cool off and reconsider his father's warning to end the budding romance, because she couldn't bear to think what would happen to her family if it continued.

Roman poked at his food. If he could manage to break up Aden and Annie, would his brother ever forgive him? Mamm reached over and removed his plate. "You're not eating anyway, and your youngest sister needs help with her homework."

Roman glanced at Arie. She was tall and skinny for a ten-year-old, and he imagined she'd always be quite thin. She shrugged apologetically, probably afraid he'd lash out at her too.

He motioned toward her room. "Get your stuff, Breezy, and let's get it done."

She smiled at his use of her pet name and took off. With an Amish name pronounced like *airy,* he always called her Windy, Breezy, or Gusty.

He watched as his siblings helped clear the table. None of them had eaten much either. He had himself to thank for that. And Aden. Annie too, for that matter.

The phone rang, and Mary and Jake ran out the front door, seeing who would arrive at the phone shanty first.

Arie set her math book and spiral notebook on the table. "I'm horrible at math. I don't know why I have to study it."

Roman flipped open the book. "Because it's our lot in life to face our stupidity and try to overcome it." He turned the pages. "Chapter twenty, right?"

Arie scooted the chair closer to him. "I think I'd be insulted, except nobody knows facing stupidity more than you."

Roman chuckled. "Do you want my help or not?"

"As opposed to failing? Definitely."

Jake rushed into the room. "Roman, it's for you."

"Me?"

"It's a girl." He grinned. "I like her too. She's funny. Mary's talking to her now. She said to tell you she's not taking no for an answer. Said she'd let the phone ring all night if she had to and at the restaurant tomorrow too."

Roman glanced at his mother, wondering if he looked as dumbfounded as he felt. It had to be Marian. He guessed it could be the girl from the wedding, but he longed for it to be Marian.

Mamm dried her hands on a dishtowel. "Go on. I'll help Arie this time."

Roman's thoughts ran wild as he wheeled himself outside and down the side ramp to the phone.

Before the accident he'd been active and strong. A benefit to his family and friends. A hard worker. A lively talker. He could bring out the humor in any situation. That man would have gone after Marian. This one was useless. Rarely anything but a burden to everyone.

He wheeled into the small shed and held out his hand for the phone.

Mary giggled. "Roman's here. I'd better go." She paused. "Ya, I'll do that. Bye." She put the phone in his hand.

"You'll do what?" Roman asked.

"Nothing." Mary ran out of the shanty.

He put the phone to his ear. "Hello?"

"I heard you went on a date the other night." Marian's voice made his heart turn a flip. He'd written her off, thinking she hated even knowing him. Every time a memory of his last interaction with her came to mind, he shoved it aside, unwilling to admit how much it hurt to have blown it with her.

"The news of rare wonders travels fast, I suppose."

She laughed. "Actually, your sister just told me."

"It wasn't really a date." Why did he tell her that? Did he care what she thought, or did he need someone to confess his sins to? He guessed it was the latter.

"No? What was it then?"

"Not sure."

"Think about it. I'll wait."

He wanted to know why she'd called, but he wasn't really in a hurry to get to the point. If she wanted to let their words create a path to trod, so did he.

She was a bit odd, and they had very odd conversations. On one hand, they were the most refreshing experiences he'd ever had. On the other, they messed with his mind and heart, confusing him and making him want more—all at the same time.

He picked up a pencil off the bench where the phone book sat and doodled on the book's cover. He couldn't do much more than stick figures.

"I'd like to say it was a real date, but in reality it was me plotting against my brother." If she didn't hate him already, he doubted his confession would cause her to start.

In the four days since he'd come home from Ernie's, the strife between Aden and him had been as thick as Aden's split pea soup, and he had to tell someone the awfulness of what he'd done. His attempts to get his brother interested in a girl other than Annie had backfired.

"Roman." Marian's voice dropped to barely audible. "Are you serious?"

The dismay in her voice heaped guilt on him. His actions had actually been more of a knee-jerk reaction. Everything in his life lately had been a failure. He hadn't been able to fix Uncle Ernie's generator. He hadn't been missed a bit at the diner, even during their busiest week. And he hadn't managed to convince his brother to end his relationship with Annie.

"I… He…" Roman put down the pencil. "Ya." There he'd told someone the absolute truth. "He's been seeing a horse-and-buggy Mennonite girl, one who's already joined the faith, and I tried to turn them against each other." He paused, and she said nothing. "Aren't you thrilled to know someone like me?"

The phone remained silent, but his admission made him almost able to tolerate himself again.

Marian had shown a hint of caring for him, along with an alluring spunk. She was like a bright, multicolored object in the middle of his drab world. But he couldn't even court her without Aden around to lift his half-limp body and haul his heavy wheelchair.

"Did you do that because she's Mennonite?"

Roman closed his eyes, still seeing his wheelchair clearly and the darkened outline of himself.

A woman couldn't carry him to the shower in the mornings when his muscles were too stiff to move. Even Uncle Ernie had trouble taking care of his needs. And asking for his help had been awkward and embarrassing.

No, like it or not, he was dependent on Aden. He couldn't survive a single day without someone's help, and the only one who really fit the bill was Aden. And until now, he'd been self-centered enough to think that Aden was just as dependent on him.

Roman tapped the pencil on the homemade bench, thinking. "I'd thought so, but maybe I'm just afraid of losing Aden." Why was he sharing the worst parts of himself with her?

He feared more than losing his brother's brawn. They'd always shared everything, and then *she* came along. Did Annie know Aden like Roman did? That was impossible. Surely even in his love stupor, Aden realized that.

"I called to tell you something." Her voice sounded different now. Maybe more distant. Maybe more intimate. He couldn't tell.

He pushed the phone book farther back on the bench. "What, you mean there's a world happening outside my own?"

She laughed, soft and whispery. "I know this sounds crazy, but I like your sarcasm."

"I have a motto: anything worth taking seriously is worth making fun of. So, what'd you call to tell me?"

"Change is inevitable, except from a vending machine."

"What?"

"Before you criticize someone, you should walk a mile in their shoes. That way, when you criticize them, you're a mile away, and you have their shoes."

He laughed. "You called to tell me corny jokes?"

"Clearly I need a new joke book." Marian laughed, and he heard a thud, as if she'd tossed the book to the ground. "Hey, you shared your stupid motto first. Besides, I've told them to everyone else. They ran away with my shoes."

"You know, I needed this weird call from you."

"Good. Then one of us got what they needed."

For the first time in way too long, Roman seriously cared about what someone else needed. How had he turned into such a selfish person? "Is there something I can do for you…keeping in mind that I'm quite limited in my abilities?"

"One thing I wanted to say is that I accept your apology."

Guilt pressed in. "I never gave one."

"But you will one day, so I decided to accept it now. And you owe Aden and that Mennonite girl one too."

"Aden's just wrong. More wrong than me. I caused an argument between him and a girl he shouldn't be seeing. He's ripping families and friends apart, and a business, and will probably tear up two communities before it's done." He paused, wondering if that justified his actions. What was that saying—two wrongs don't make a right? "But I'm really sorry I yelled at you. I was embarrassed about breaking the water pump. And I wanted to turn it into a fight with you so you'd walk away."

"There are two theories to arguing with a woman, and neither one works."

"Ya, they get over being angry and call anyway."

She laughed. "So tell me, do you feel better than you did before we talked?"

"A lot."

"But neither of us is moving. We're being still, and we both feel better…because there is so much more to every person than what we can do physically."

Her words stirred him, and he wanted to believe her, to believe he had all he needed in order to be someone's other half. Arguments rose inside him, lashing against her romantic views. A few minutes of talking, however great, did not make up for all the lack he faced daily.

"That's what I called to say. I'd better go, Roman. I just needed to say my piece, and I needed closure for us. I figured I might die of old age if I waited on you to reach out first."

He didn't want to hang up the phone or find closure. Marian seemed to understand him—and she wasn't totally turned off by his disability. He wanted to ask if he could call her sometime. But he couldn't get past what would lie down the road, beyond the entertaining phone calls and jokes. "Bye, Roman."

"Bye." He hung up the phone, reeling with thoughts of how weird and exhilarating Marian was.

What he'd done—or tried to do—to Aden weighed on him. But even as his conscience bothered him, his mind justified his actions and searched for another way to break up the two.

Some things, like a family business, were more important than a budding relationship that was forbidden for solid reasons.

Thirteen

Aden knocked on Moses's door. Two nights ago Aden's Daed had insisted he never see Annie again. He'd been taking time to think.

There was a lot against them, but the bottom line was that to continue seeing her, however secret they could keep it, would be selfish on his part. And dangerous for her and for his family's business. He needed to face her and tell her the truth.

Steeling his resolve, he knocked on Moses's door again, hoping he'd be out and Annie would answer. No such luck.

"Aden." Annie's grandfather appeared surprised to see him. This man had worked tirelessly beside Aden after the farming accident, and despite Moses's gruff side, it'd once seemed that he truly liked Aden. But as the elderly man held on firmly to the door, blocking Aden from seeing inside his home, it was apparent that Moses no longer felt that way.

"Everything okay at the diner?" Moses asked.

"Ya. D-denki."

Looking perplexed, Moses motioned. "Well, come on in."

Aden entered the house, hoping to catch sight of Annie. He saw no sign of her.

Moses flipped a switch, filling the kitchen with artificial light. Aden thought it made the room feel more like a business than a home. He wondered what it was like to live in a house without kerosene lanterns and a wood-burning cookstove adding a touch of warmth to the place.

Moses poured himself a cup of coffee from the electric pot. He held up an empty cup, silently asking if Aden wanted him to fill it. Aden shook his head. Moses went to the table and took a seat, gesturing for Aden to do the same. "So what brings you here, boy?" He peered at Aden's wringing hands. "Your Daed need me to help at the diner this week?"

"No. I c-came to talk about Annie."

Moses's eyes narrowed. "Why?"

"I…" Aden took a deep breath to calm his nerves. "I've b-been seeing her."

"I figured that out already. You kept your hands off my granddaughter, Aden?"

"C-completely."

Moses studied him, sizing him up and perhaps trying to decide if he was being honest. "Gut. That helps. Now, are you here to set things right between our families or make them worse?"

Aden fought to say the words that needed to be said, not the ones he wanted to say. "M-make them right."

"Gut. I always did believe in you, Aden. You know that, right?"

"Ya." He never doubted that Moses believed in him, in his ability to meet the needs of the diner as a scrawny teen and provide for his family. Aden used to rely on Moses's confidence to get through the darkest of days.

Moses took his mug by the handle. "She ain't been feeling too well lately. Hasn't done much of anything the last couple of days. 'Cept for hanging out with the chickens."

Aden had to take the blame for that. He never should have let her think there could be anything but friendship between them.

"She's out there right now, matter of fact." Moses stood and pulled a wicker basket from a low cupboard. "Might as well make yourself useful. Any eggs you find you can have for the restaurant." He shoved the basket into Aden's hands. "Shouldn't take more'n a few minutes to gather eggs and deliver a message."

Aden followed the noisy sound of clucking chickens to a grassy yard surrounded by a wire fence. Annie stood beside the coop, leaning against the wall and petting the wings of a black rooster with a bright red comb. She stared beyond the fence in the direction of the cherry tree orchard.

When he cleared his throat, she turned abruptly, her eyes wide. The startled rooster spread his wings, cackled, and flew into the little wooden house.

"Hello, Aden."

Her words were familiar, but they had no hint of the warmth he'd grown used to hearing in her voice. However, he hadn't come here to make amends. He'd come to set things right. Still, she had to be willing to hear him—despite all he'd never be able to say.

Since she didn't come closer to him, he went inside the fence and held up the basket. "I c-came for some e-e-e-." He hadn't stuttered this much since she showed up at the diner that first day. He tried to think of a tune that would help him express what he really wanted to say. But no music played in his mind or heart.

Without a word she walked into the coop. He followed her, feeling like a lying hypocrite. How could he say good-bye when all he could think about was building a life with her?

She motioned to a row of nests. "Check the ones on the left side. They should have something for you." She propped herself against the wall and crossed her arms.

Aden stared at the few hens sitting comfortably on their nests. He hadn't a clue how to retrieve eggs from underneath a chicken. Would they peck at him for trying to steal their potential babies?

"What are you waiting for?" Annie said. "They're not going to put their eggs in the basket for you."

He tentatively approached the calmest-looking one. Her beady eyes seemed to stare at him, gauging his every move.

"Maybe my customers d-don't need e-eggs this weekend after all." He cleared his throat and put a tune to his words. "Ya, that's it. Didn't we read something last week about them being high in cholesterol? I might be doing my patrons a favor by not having eggs on the menu for a while. Or anything made with eggs."

A glance at Annie told him his song and his hesitation amused her. It was the first trace of a smile he'd seen on her face since he'd walked up. He hated the idea of telling her they had to go separate ways, but he was determined to do it under friendly circumstances.

He maintained eye contact with the hen as he slipped his hand under her warm feathers and felt around. His fingertips encountered something hard and round. He wrapped his hand around it and inched it out. In his grip he saw a large beige egg.

Invigorated by his success, he flashed a grin at Annie.

She laughed. "Congratulations. You got one. But you'll need a lot more than one for tomorrow's crowd."

She was softening toward him. Good. He might be able to say what he came to tell her after all.

But by the time he'd finished depriving the hens of their eggs, she'd gone back outside. He set the basket on a stool beside the coop and walked toward her. As he did, he heard a loud cough from inside the house. A glance that way revealed Moses watching through the window. Surely Aden's allotted few minutes were up—and then some.

"Annie…" How could he tell her everything that was in his heart in such a short time? He couldn't exactly break into song with her Daadi watching.

"It's all right, Aden," she said softly without turning around to look at him. "I was silly to think you cared for me."

"But I d-do care." He needed to explain everything. But he couldn't do that with her grandfather watching them, counting the minutes.

With his back to the house, hoping Moses couldn't see, he touched Annie's arm and gently turned her to face him. He gazed into her eyes, praying that she'd look into his heart and read all the emotions he was still trying to sort out himself. "The sacrifice f-f-for you is huge." He whispered the words. "Massive. Destructive."

Her eyes misted. "I know. And you could have that other girl with no trouble piled onto that relationship."

He longed to explain what Roman had lied about, but it'd take too many words. "She's n-not important."

Annie studied him.

"Ch-choosing." He hoped she was familiar with that tradition.

"Oh." She appeared to understand what he was saying, but the hurt didn't fade from her eyes. "Daadi Moses let you come talk to me, so I guess you're here to say good-bye."

No part of him wanted to say good-bye. Maybe he was letting the requirements of others influence him too much. Had he even asked her what she wanted? Suddenly unwilling to walk away with only broken dreams, he reconsidered his plans. "Listen, Annie." He glanced back at the house, wondering if he was making a mistake. Was it right to ask her to give up so much? It didn't matter if he left his community or she left hers; either way, she'd lose the respect of her church and family. Still, it seemed right to let her choose. "I'm in love with you."

Her eyes grew wide.

He took a step back. This wasn't the time for an emotional reaction of some kind.

"Just think about the sacrifice b-being together would t-take, and then we'll talk."

"Tonight?"

Guilt stole his ability to think. He'd told Moses he'd come to set things right, and now he was making plans to secretly meet up with Annie. "Ya."

Fourteen

A quarter moon played hide-and-seek behind the clouds as Annie wandered through her grandfather's cherry tree orchard, inspecting the tiny buds on the dark branches. Any day now those buds would start to open, and soon the entire field would be transformed into a wonderland of pink-and-white cherry blossoms, filling the air with their sweet aroma. She admired one tree after another as she made her way down the rows.

Moses had been kind and gentle throughout the evening and had kissed the top of her head before going to bed. His tenderness added to her confusion concerning what to tell Aden. She couldn't bear the thought of having to choose between her beloved grandfather and Aden.

She spotted Aden walking toward her, flanked by budding cherry trees, and she thought her heart might leap out of her chest. His steady countenance spoke of inner strength buried beneath a lifetime of inability to speak his feelings. She'd seen beyond those layers into a soul that was rich in compassion, faith, and staunch loyalty—to his family and to God. How she longed to help him bring those qualities to the surface where others could see what she saw in him.

"I'm glad you're here," she whispered into the night air, silent but for the trilling of insects and the rush of water over stones.

His lips curved into a smile. "M-me too."

They strolled along the trees in silence.

Aden picked up a stick. "We would have t-to weather a lot to be together, and it's okay if you d-don't want to go through that."

Annie moved a low hanging branch out of the way, trying to draw the courage to say the words she needed to say. "Aden…"

He stopped and looked into her face. The moonlight reflected on his amber-colored eyes.

"I need more time before I know what to do," she forced out.

He seemed unsure, but he nodded. "Okay."

"It's one thing to want something and another matter to be willing to destroy lives to get it."

"Very true."

Unable to look into his sorrowful eyes a moment longer, she focused on the nearest cherry tree, counting the number of buds on a single branch.

Aden moved beside her and intertwined his fingers with hers and squeezed gently. "But their wants aren't the only ones that m-matter."

"Even Roman's?"

He pulled his hand free slowly, as if it were the last thing on earth he wanted to do. He didn't answer.

How could she come between two brothers who loved and needed each other so much? And how would the rest of the Zook family be affected? She couldn't expect Aden to leave his parents, his siblings, his business, and his faith for her...and she'd never ask him to. Such a thing would be a terrible wound, especially for Ellen. Annie couldn't break her heart like that.

She didn't care as much about the hurt this might cause her own mother. But what about her grandfather? Like any Plain man, Moses intended for his family to remain true to the faith they were raised in.

No matter how hard she tried, she could see no solution. But now she knew what her heart had known since she was fifteen—ignoring all family obstacles, Aden was the one for her.

"Enough seriousness." Annie grabbed a flat rock. "Let's go to the widest part of the creek, and I bet I can make a rock skip the most times before it reaches the other side." She tossed the rock up and then caught it, daring him to try to outdo her ability at the game.

Fifteen

*E*llen's husband snored softly as she got up. Unable to sleep, she slid into her housecoat and shoes before going downstairs. They'd worked so hard to keep their family intact, and now love threatened to rip it apart? It just didn't seem right.

She went to the refrigerator and poured herself a cup of milk. A noise coming from the master bedroom caught her attention, and she went toward it. She and David slept upstairs in Aden and Roman's old bedroom. The master bedroom, the one on the main floor with its own bathroom, was like a lot of things since the accident—it had to be given up for Roman's sake.

Roman wheeled out of his room, wearing boxers and a T-shirt. His eyes met hers, and even in the dark she could see the taut lines across his face. She moved past him to peer into the bedroom. Aden wasn't in bed. Roman's bed was a wreck, and everything that had been on his side table was now scattered on the floor. "Is Aden home?"

Roman shrugged, but clearly he'd managed to get into his wheelchair by himself. Apparently, he hadn't been in bed long enough for his muscles to become intolerably stiff.

"So suddenly you want to protect your brother?"

"What I want is for things to go back to the way they were before *she* arrived."

Grief mixed with raw panic, making it hard for her to breathe. They'd have no way to make a living without the diner. "I need some fresh air." She went to the door and stepped onto the porch, reminding herself to hold on to hope.

Roman came outside and parked his wheelchair near the porch swing. "What Aden's doing isn't right, Mamm."

She sat and rocked, asking God to give her the right words. "We don't need to talk about him right now. I want to know what's going on with you."

Roman stared at the stars for a long moment. "I'm like you—just worried about what Aden is doing, the problems it'll cause for all of us."

"I think that's only part of it. If I dragged him back here right now…if he ended it with Annie tonight, it wouldn't solve what's going on between you two. It'd probably make things worse for a long, long time."

"It's so unfair."

"You think what's happening to Aden is fair?"

He stared off into the night sky. "Aden's shut me out. I'm gone a week, and he replaces me with Annie—and what he can be with her."

"That's not really surprising. You're twenty-two years old. All siblings go through a time of separation as they get older and are ready to go their separate ways, start their own families."

Roman rubbed the smooth armrest of the porch swing. "After the accident I…I thought he'd always be here, him and me together."

"It was bound to happen sooner or later. I'm holding out for it to happen with a nice Amish girl, but either way he will eventually leave the nest."

He looked at his mother with tear-filled eyes. "But what about me?"

Ellen leaned back and folded her arms. "What about you?"

"I can't build a life with any woman," he choked out.

"You don't know that. Not yet, anyway. It takes more time for some people to find a mate. I think you'll find a girl who sees the best in you—if you don't ruin the possibility with all your bitterness first."

He scoffed. "Like Linda saw the best in me?"

Pinpricks of angst ran over her skin. He'd been dating a lovely girl before the accident. She'd stayed by his side at the hospital, holding his hand, whispering words of encouragement to him. But when the doctor said his injuries were permanent and he'd never walk again, her visits became more sporadic. Her attitude toward him grew distant. Shortly after he returned home in a wheelchair, she told him she couldn't see him anymore. Roman hadn't pursued another girl since.

"What about the girl at Gideon and Mattie's wedding?"

"I only did that to get Aden to spend time with someone besides Annie." He shrugged. "And maybe I wanted to cause some trouble between them."

"Maybe?"

"Let's talk about something else, okay?"

"Well…tell me about that date."

"We were having a pretty good time…until she saw how much work Aden exerted putting my wheelchair into the carriage and lifting me onto the seat. Then all she could do was stare at my mangled legs."

She longed to promise him that, given time, he'd find a girl, but that might not ever happen, and she wouldn't lie. "It's possible that one day you'll find someone who accepts you unconditionally. Who decides that your spinal cord injury isn't too much to live with. Someone who sees past the chair and likes you for who you are."

He intertwined his fingers, staring at them. "I only know one woman who fits that description."

She leaned forward. "That's a start. Who?"

His lips tugged upward a bit, as if he was fighting a smile. "Uncle Ernie's neighbor, Marian Lee."

Marian Lee. The name rang a bell. "Is she the one who called here a week or so ago?"

"That's her."

"Isn't she the one who wrote you all those letters after the accident?"

"Ya." His voice carried a softness she hadn't heard in a long time.

"As I recall, you didn't answer most of them. Have you called her since she called here?"

"I'm going to bed." He rolled toward the door and waited. It was his way of saying the subject was closed.

She stood and opened the screen and solid door for him. "Well, maybe you should write or call her."

"I don't think so, Mamm. We landed in a good place the other night when she called. I'm leaving well enough alone." He rolled into the house and toward his room.

"Roman."

He stopped and turned back to her.

She put a hand on each arm of his chair and kissed his cheek. "You have to face your fears, or you'll paralyze your life. You can become someone who doesn't resent his brother falling in love. Who doesn't try to manipulate him for selfish purposes. You can be someone who has the courage to try to be in a relationship or who has the peace to live single. And probably without Aden at some point. But to become that man, it'll take reaching for the unfathomable strength of the One who created you."

He headed for his room. "You want me to draw strength from a God who left me like this?"

"Do you need any help?" she asked, knowing she wasn't up to the task of aiding him with much.

"No, but thanks." With his back to her, he waved his hand. "If anything gets too hard, I'll just pray about it and wait for an answer."

Weary of battles, Ellen waited outside her son's room until the silence told her he'd gotten into bed. She went out back, watching for Aden to return. Leaning against a huge oak tree, she prayed for wisdom and soaked in the sounds and scents of spring. The smell of freshly plowed earth. The low-pitched, slow call of the chuck-will's-widow. But she couldn't fully enjoy any of them. Not with such tension between her boys.

Finally she saw Aden walking through the back field. Gathering her robe and her courage, she went across the lawn to meet him.

When he spotted her, he stopped in his tracks for a moment. The pain and confusion she saw in him ran as deep as what she'd seen in Roman.

He lowered his head. "What am I g-going to do?"

Ellen wished she knew. Wished there was an easy answer. All she wanted was for her sons to be happy. "Sometimes temporary happiness results in long-term misery. We're all tempted to go our own way at times, Aden."

"It's not l-like that."

"How can you be so sure?"

"How d-did you know you'd love every child you c-conceived before you ever held us in your arms?"

"That's different."

"Answer m-me."

She ran her fingertips from her forehead back to her ponytail, suddenly aware that her hair wasn't pinned up properly and she didn't have on her prayer Kapp. "I just knew."

"Ya, m-me too."

They walked back to the house together and sat on the back steps.

"Son, if you continue on this path, there's heartache in that too. So whether you keep seeing Annie or not, there's going to be a lot of pain. You need to choose whether to suffer the anguish of ending things with her now or to experience all the grief a relationship with her would cause for yourself, her, and everyone in both families for years to come."

They sat there for several long minutes without saying a word. Ellen hoped that God would speak to her son's heart beyond anything she could say to him.

"I know you can't see it right now"—she weighed her words carefully as she watched clouds move across the sky—"but there are other girls out there for you."

Aden stood. "Good night, Mamm."

He went inside, leaving her to face her hypocrisy. She didn't want him to find someone else for his own good, but for hers. And her family's. And Moses's.

Sixteen

*A*nnie strolled through the orchard, the cherry blossoms now in full bloom. Normally the sight and the smell overwhelmed her with delight. But not tonight.

She'd been thrilled at the opportunity to share this special experience with Aden. He'd met her here every night for a week, watching the tiny buds grow, then begin to open, then pop out wide as the abundant blossoms took over every tree.

While they walked, they talked about everything from their favorite pastimes to remarkable meals and recipes. They discussed recent articles in the newspaper, including what would happen at the diner once the closest plaza on the turnpike shut down. They shared what they believed. They connected so easily, like gliding on ice, only more breathtaking. Occasionally he sang his thoughts to her, but more and more he'd been communicating without a tune or a stutter. Every night her heart soared a little higher.

And Daadi hadn't a clue about her late-night walks.

On Sunday they'd allowed their conversations to touch on the future. He asked her again if she'd decided whether she could go through all it'd take for them to be together. She shook her head and changed the subject, turning from the future to focus on the now—concrete things like weddings they'd attended and the price the newly married couples were paying for houses.

Then on Monday night Aden hadn't shown. She waited as long as she could before returning home. He hadn't come on Tuesday either. Or last night.

Annie yanked a twig of cherry blossoms off the nearest tree. Roman—he was most likely behind Aden's absence the last few nights. Though Aden claimed he didn't care what his brother thought, she knew that wasn't true. Even without their unique circumstances, as twins, Aden and Roman would always have a tight bond.

As she breathed in the cherry blossom aroma, she realized that the deepest part of her never believed she and Aden had a real chance.

But she wasn't ready to give up on them. Was he? Was that why he wasn't here?

Tears slid down her cheeks, and she broke into sobs.

Finally accepting that Aden wasn't coming again tonight, Annie shuffled back toward the house. She had to figure a way to see him. If he'd given up on them, he needed to look her in the eyes and say so.

<hr />

Annie's insides trembled as she neared Zook's Diner. As soon as Daadi had returned to the field after lunch, she'd headed this way. Her chores were done, and she'd be back before he returned home for the evening meal. But the distance from Daadi's to here had never seemed so vast. At the same time, two miles weren't very far to travel to face one's future.

That's what she was doing, wasn't it—coming to discover if Aden cared enough to keep seeing her?

At fifteen she'd known that if she and Aden ever tried to cross the forbidden lines, the pressure that loved ones would put on them to end the relationship would be powerful. And that was just the first step. If she and Aden ignored their families, the church and the community would be informed, and even more pressure would be applied—a lot more.

She'd spent years consoling herself that staying in their own faith communities was the right thing for her and Aden to do. But she couldn't believe that lie any longer. She'd fallen in love. She might have doubted what she wanted from Aden before arriving in Apple Ridge three weeks ago, but she'd never be able to deny it again.

Maybe she was a fool to hope he could ever love her enough to go against what his family and church demanded of him. She walked around to the back entrance and went straight into the kitchen. Aden stood at the stove, flipping hamburgers and bacon. The aromas made her stomach growl, reminding her that she hadn't eaten since last night's supper.

He tossed a patty onto a toasted bun, added lettuce, tomato, and a strip of bacon, squirted condiments, and slapped the other half of the bun on top. When he turned to pull a wire basket full of french fries out of the deep fryer, he caught sight of Annie. He froze, his hand inches from the handle.

"I need you to tell me what's going on, Aden."

He pulled the fries from the grease and dumped them into the stainless steel container. After salting them, he put some on the plate beside the burger—a couple of them missed and fell to the floor. Without bothering to pick them up, Aden put the plate on the pass-through and tapped the bell.

Leaving an unfilled order slip on the counter, Aden turned off the stove and ushered Annie to a back corner of the kitchen, out of sight of the pass-through.

"It's not a g-good idea for you to be here," he whispered.

"I couldn't let you disappear on me like that. Do you know how it feels to be alone and waiting for someone who doesn't show up? It's miserable."

"I d-don't want you to f-feel that way. But sneaking around…it's wrong. We b-both know it. And you n-never even want to t-talk about what it will take to be together."

As much as she wanted to deny what he'd said, she knew it was true. "I can't bear to think of hurting our families or of what Daadi will do to your business. I just want to be together, Aden."

"M-me too. B-but that's n-not enough, is it?"

"Aden?" Roman's voice filtered through the kitchen. "Aden, where are you?"

He left Annie and walked up to his brother.

"Moses is here. Says he needs to talk to you."

Annie's heart pounded with fear. She didn't want to be yelled at in front of a diner full of people.

Aden pulled the white apron over his head, tossed it onto a counter, and strode out of the kitchen into the seating area.

Annie tried to think of the best thing to do. Should she go out the back way so her grandfather wouldn't see her? She couldn't possibly make it home before he did. Eventually he would ask where she'd been, and she'd have to tell him the truth. The minutes ticked by, and her head ached from the rush of blood pounding in her ears.

"M-Moses, wait," she heard Aden call.

The kitchen door flung open, and Daadi's frame filled the doorway. "You need to go home. Now."

Aden moved between Annie and Moses, as if unsure what her grandfather would do next.

"Yes, Daadi." Though she longed for another glance at Aden, she didn't dare as she went toward the back door. It was all she could do not to throw herself into Aden's arms as she neared him.

"I don't mean my home," Moses informed her. "I mean yours."

"What?" She stopped short, struggling for air.

"I've already hired a driver. He's waiting out front to take you back to the farm. As soon as you've packed your things, he'll drive you home."

"But, Daadi—"

He gestured toward the door. "Now, Annie."

She hesitated.

"Do I need to remind you that this place has electricity because I remain a business partner?"

His threat worked its way through her, leaving her dizzy and weak. Her knees gave way, but before she collapsed onto the floor, strong arms caught her and kept her on her feet. She looked up at Aden, whose misty eyes told her he hated what was happening, but he had no solutions.

She longed for him to promise he'd wait for her, like her Daadi had waited for her grandmother Esther. Annie didn't expect Aden to buy fields and plant cherry trees on them. But he could at least tell her he'd write while they were apart, to keep their relationship alive until years from now when her Daadi's heart softened and he wasn't so set against them.

Aden helped her stand, but he didn't utter a single word. Moses waited, and she was grateful he didn't jerk Aden away from her.

Her head spun. "Aden?"

He backed away from her, and her heart shattered. When a horn tooted, she ran out the back door of the diner, grateful for a vehicle that would get her away from here.

Seventeen

*A*den sat on one of the many benches set up in his own home for the Easter Sunday service. The bishop held out his hands. "Let's pray."

The gentle noise of two hundred people quietly shifting from their seats to a kneeling position reminded him of his many years of living Old Order Amish. He prayed for Annie, asking that at least she would find happiness. But he physically ached from missing her.

When the prayer time was over, everyone stood for the reading of Scripture. He tried to listen, but he kept asking God the same question over and over—if he or Annie left their church after taking a vow, would He forgive them?

The bishop closed the Bible, and everyone took a seat. A visiting preacher stood and began singing "Neither Do I Condemn Thee." It was a favorite Easter song that wasn't in the *Ausbund.* He, along with everyone else, had learned it in English while attending school.

With no condemnation but only freedom to experience…

He'd sung it many times, but this time the words washed over him as he sang.

We can grow in our spiritual life and be strong...

Aden poured out his heart in prayer while singing the words, and suddenly, like sunrise after a winter's night, he knew that he had no sinful motive for leaving his people and that God would not condemn him for it. Powerful thoughts about loyalty and faithfulness ran through him, but, oddly, every single one seemed to point to the fact that he had the freedom in Christ, if not among his own people, to be forgiven for breaking his word and to pursue Annie.

One brick wall that separated him from Annie crumbled to the ground. But only one. He probably faced half a dozen more.

This morning, as dawn was breaking, he'd gone for a walk, meandering on and on until he found himself in Moses's orchard. The cherry blossoms, which had just begun to bloom when he saw them last, were already starting to fade and fall off the trees. He'd missed the brief window of time during which he could have enjoyed their full effect.

Had he also missed his chance to win Annie's heart?

It was getting dark when Roman finally got away from the church crowd and went toward his bedroom. He grumbled to himself about

Aden disappearing right after the church meal and leaving him to help Mary hide eggs all afternoon. He'd been tempted to hide the lot of them in a pile of fresh dung.

Because it was Easter, his mother had made a few special items for the after-service meal—pickled red beets with dozens of boiled eggs added. The eggs were a pink color, and people seemed so pleased at their beauty and taste. Later that afternoon the older children and some adults hid Easter eggs for the younger ones to find. The Amish didn't include the Easter bunny, but most allowed for egg hunts and chocolate candy. Thankfully, the excitement over eating pink pickled eggs and hiding decorated eggs was over for the year.

Once in his room, he saw no sign of Aden.

Good. Finally he had a few minutes alone to see what his brother had been up to. Whenever he had a free second, Aden had a pad of paper out. And lately he hadn't been willing to show Roman anything, which only made him more curious. What was Aden doing that he didn't want even his own brother to see?

Perhaps he wasn't drawing at all. Could Aden be writing letters to Annie? If they were still communicating, their feelings for each other would grow stronger, and who knew where that would lead?

Roman had seen his brother stash sketchbooks in his footlocker for years. Whenever Roman had questioned him about the contents of his footlocker lately, Aden had told him to mind his own business.

What else might his brother be keeping in his private storage? Perhaps love letters from a Mennonite girl? Roman gingerly lifted the lid of the footlocker and peeked inside. He saw no envelopes—just neat stacks of sketchbooks, the top one sitting slightly askew. Roman reached in and picked it up.

This was the one his brother had been working on most recently. He recognized the cover—which had been slammed closed countless times whenever Roman came into the room. Unable to squelch his curiosity, he opened the cover. On the first page was a tiny tree in the middle of a large field, a circle of dirt around its trunk. He turned the page. In the second drawing, there were two trees—one just like the first, the other a little bigger. As he flipped through pages, each one had a new tree among progressively larger versions of the previous ones.

Finally he came to a sketch of a field full of stark, bare trees. In the next drawing, the trees had tiny buds. After that, just-opening blooms.

The last picture stole his next heartbeat. The page was covered with vibrant green trees bearing an abundance of cherry blossoms. The delicate shades of pink and vibrant tinges of red made the picture seem so real he could practically smell the orchard. Aden must have put a lot of time and work into this one.

Though Roman would have loved to linger on this drawing, he wondered what came next.

He set the book aside and picked up another one. In it he found drawings of Annie. Some were of just her face or a portion of her face. A few were of her hands, the back of her head with her Mennonite prayer Kapp, or a closeup of her eyes. In others she was standing in the orchard, sitting at the counter in their diner, picking up plates from the pass-through.

Shaking off feelings of guilt, Roman dug deeper in the footlocker, suddenly hoping to find drawings that didn't have something to do with Annie. But book after book was filled with her. Aden had been drawing pictures of her as far back as the year Roman and his Daed were injured, when Annie and her grandfather had helped Aden keep the diner running during their rehab.

He discovered pictures of Mamm, Daed, Roman, and their siblings throughout various stages. Some depicted Christmas mornings, church baptisms, or weddings. But Roman couldn't find even one of any other girl.

Was this how Aden had always felt—that Annie was the only one for him? He'd never said anything. Never pursued her.

Roman's blood rushed through his body, making him feel lightheaded. Aden was trapped too?

Guilt mixed with self-doubt. He'd been selfish to try to keep his brother to himself instead of helping him find ways around the obstacles he faced.

His heart pounded, and he had to talk to someone. No, he had to talk to Marian. She was the only one with enough guts to tell it like it was. He put the sketchbooks back in the chest and wheeled himself through the house. He shouldn't call her on a Sunday, but he went straight to the phone shanty.

He scrolled through all the numbers that came up on the caller ID, hoping her number was still listed. She'd called him a little over three weeks ago. If they'd received too many calls since then, it wouldn't still be there.

Finally he saw it. Vernon Lee. Her father. He punched the Dial

Display button and waited. Five. Six. Seven rings. One thing about the Amish and their phone shanties, they set their phones to ring as many times as possible before the answering machine picked up.

"You've reached the Lees. Leave a message."

"Uh…" Roman couldn't think of what to say. She was probably gone to a singing. That's what the Amish singles did on Sunday nights, and some lucky guy would take her home on a long, scenic route. "This is Roman calling for Marian. If you will, please tell her I called. Denki." He hung up. It was never easy leaving a message for a girl who lived at home with lots of siblings. The most he could hope for was that someone remembered to give her the message.

He sat in the dark shed, wishing he could pray. Wishing it made a difference. It'd been so long. Years, actually. If he could speak to God, he'd—

The phone rang, and he grabbed it. "Hello."

"Hi."

"Marian, I…I thought you'd be at a singing."

"I wouldn't waste my time, not around here anyway. And Mamm wouldn't let me go elsewhere with it being Easter. What's on your mind?"

"I needed to talk to someone."

"Then talk."

"I'm going crazy here. I wanted to break up Aden and Annie, and now I'm starting to think that maybe they were meant to be together. That makes no sense. Why would God want me broken and want to give Aden a girl that will destroy the family business and the family?"

"Wait. You're mad at God because you think He wants you broken? Golly, Roman, so you think every time someone gets a virus or a bug bite or loses their kerosene lighter, it's God doing it?"

"He could prevent those things."

"Open your eyes, Roman. After Christ was born and Herod killed all those babies while trying to kill Jesus, it wasn't God choosing to devastate those mothers. He brought salvation into the world, and a selfish, power-hungry man thought he could stop God. I don't know why God didn't just wipe out Herod. I do know that scene is an image of the constant battle between good and evil—and it takes place all the time. For now. Read Hebrews chapter two, verse eight. See if you see what I do. I believe God is telling us that even though everything is under His feet, we don't see that as our full reality right now."

Roman couldn't answer. It was all too much to think about. He could read that chapter and verse she'd mentioned a thousand times, and he knew he'd never figure out God. But could he believe that his brokenness wasn't plotted by God?

That aside, one thing in all she'd said stood out very clearly. In this mess with Aden and Annie, he was Herod—a selfish, mortal man who thought he could control his future.

"Hey," Marian whispered, "you still there?"

"Barely." His eyes burned with tears. "Can we talk about something else? I think I may like that stupid joke book more than I thought."

"Ya? Well, remember this, a day without sunshine is like...night. Oh, and I read this on a bumper sticker the other day: what happens if you get scared half to death twice?"

He chuckled, feeling closer to God than he had in a really long time. He knew he and Marian would never be more than phone friends, but it seemed to him that he could at least ask about her life once in a while. "Hey, what was Easter like over there?"

Eighteen

*A*nnie reached into the laundry basket of clean, wet clothes and pulled out a twin-sized bedsheet. Warm rays of light stretched across the land like angelic fingers from heaven as she hung item after item on the clothesline. The scene did not match her mood, but she kept plodding forward.

The phone rang, jolting her. She refused to drop the wet shirt into the basket and run for the house. She'd given up on Aden calling her. If he hadn't called or written in the three weeks since she'd come home, he wasn't going to. How could he? If he reached out to her, her grandfather would withdraw his partnership in the diner.

She'd reapplied for her job at the market, and the owner said he hoped to call her next week with an opening for her. He wouldn't call on a Saturday, not on the busiest market day of the week.

"Annie." Mamm stepped onto the back porch. "Phone."

Her heart turned a flip, foolishly unconvinced to give up on Aden. "Who is it?"

"It's your Daadi."

She didn't want to talk to him, but she needed to at least be an adult about it and tell him so. Leaving the items behind, she hurried into the house and picked up the corded phone. "Hello."

"Happy birthday." He broke into singing a crazy, out-of-tune version of the birthday song. She'd forgotten she turned twenty today. This annual ritual always seemed out of character for him, a lot like his planting all those cherry trees. After a full round of the song, he stopped.

"Denki."

"Feel any older?"

"No. And it was nice of you to remember, but I'm not interested in—"

"Hey." He interrupted, sounding more hurt than angry. "You were wrong to disobey me, to ignore the vow you've taken. Actually, it's me who should be avoiding you."

"Okay. That works too, I suppose. Bye."

"Annie, wait."

"No, Daadi. You embarrassed me in front of everyone and threatened to ruin the Zooks. But I'm the only one who's wrong? Why, because you say so? If Mammi Esther had been Amish, would you have walked away from her?"

His momentary silence indicated that she'd struck a nerve.

"You've taken a vow, Annie. You can't walk away from that."

"Why? Is that the unpardonable sin? It's not ideal, and I confess it's wrong. I'll make sure I'm never again so foolish as to take another vow I can't keep. But I'm not the only one who has some responsibility concerning that vow. I was sixteen, and you and Mamm were pressuring me to take that step. I wanted to please both of you. And although Aden had done nothing to encourage my feelings for him, I cared deeply for him even then, and I foolishly thought I could free my heart of him if I started dating. But I couldn't date unless I took the vow first. All that aside, I believe God would forgive me. Not so sure about man though, including my own Daadi Moses."

His breathing came with short, choppy sounds, as if...he were tempted to weep. It made no sense to try to reason with him. Even if he changed his mind completely, she and Aden were done. Young plants shriveled due to the intense heat of parental disapproval. If they couldn't withstand that, they'd never have survived the condemnation of their churches or communities.

Mamm put her arm around Annie's shoulders. "You've said enough now." Tears brimmed in her mother's eyes. "When I'm through here, we need to talk. Go finish getting laundry on the line." She took the phone.

Her mother hadn't known about Annie's transgressions in Apple Ridge, not until she overheard this conversation. When Annie had returned home, Mamm let her in and took her traveling bag, quietly mentioning the sadness in Annie's eyes. Annie didn't want to talk about it, and her mother hadn't pried.

Now that Mamm knew a little more, there'd be no avoiding a conversation. As Annie went outside, her mother was speaking quietly, almost respectfully, to her Daed. Annie hadn't heard that happen in years, and she hoped the chat ended without their usual arguments.

It'd been just seven weeks since her mother had asked her to leave Seneca Falls. But so much had changed inside her that it seemed like a lifetime ago. She hadn't been able to stop thinking about Aden. She couldn't go back, and she struggled to move forward.

Annie returned to hanging laundry, and soon Mamm came out the door. She grabbed a pillowcase out of the basket and snapped it in the wind before putting it on the line. "I know we have our troubles, Annie, but I love you." Mamm's voice cracked. "Tell me what's going on between you and your Daadi."

Annie explained everything, including her sneakiness and heartbreak.

"I was nearly three years younger than you are now when I thought desire was the same as love. Unfortunately, that foolishness is what led to the last ten years of single parenting."

Annie's throat closed up tight. Her mother never talked about what drew her and Daed together or the trials of raising a family alone. Daed had left them almost ten years ago, just a few months after Erla was born. Annie never knew why. And she learned quickly not to ask. But whatever he was doing, he sent money on the first of every month.

"Your grandfather walked in on us kissing." Mamm wiped a stray tear. "Your dad and I…were on the bed…fully clothed, mind you, but your Daadi Moses was furious. Soon rumors about me were flying through the community. I know now where those rumors started. Your dad had bragged about us making out on my bed to some of his close friends, and they told a few people, and so on. The ensuing scandal was awful. The church leaders came to see me, and your Daadi

Moses insisted I get married. Later, when the marriage went sour, I blamed your Daadi Moses for making me marry your dad, but the truth was, at the time I wanted to marry him. I'm no longer sure what your father wanted."

Annie thought about how respectful Aden had been of her people's boundaries, barely taking her hand into his one time. Never trying to kiss her or put his arms around her. Even so, he was considered completely inappropriate for her.

She couldn't imagine her Daed having any emotion other than grumpiness. He'd seemed miserable about everything. Was that why Mamm let her children do pretty much anything they wanted and let them avoid Daadi Moses? Did she want them to make their own choices because they had to live with them?

Annie shifted to look into her mother's face. "Did you love him?"

"I thought so. But the truth is, I never took the time to get to know him. I knew how I felt when I was in his arms, and I let that blind me to everything else." She ran her hand down a hanging sheet. "Have you made that same mistake?"

Annie's insides quaked as they spoke of such delicate matters. "No. I've never been in his arms, and I've only dreamed of kissing him."

"You were only gone a few weeks."

"I've always liked everything about Aden—who he is, how he handles life, what he believes. Over the years I've had some strong feelings for him. This time...our friendship changed. It was as if I pulled a familiar box of oranges off the shelf and discovered it was full of apples."

Mamm gently took her by the shoulders and stared at her before embracing her. "I'm so proud of you." She held her for a while and then took a step back. "Is it over between you and…"

"Aden Zook."

"Ah, a Zook. I remember his father back in the day. Always nice and encouraging. Even when the rumors were at their worst and your Daadi wouldn't speak to me, David and his then-girlfriend Ellen went out of their way to be polite and kind. They'd invite me to come visit at one of their homes. I never took them up on the offer, mostly out of guilt for the shame heaped on me, but it meant a lot. I hear they've had their share of troubles in recent years too."

Annie nodded. "They have, and I won't make it worse. It's over between me and Aden."

"And your heart is broken."

She nodded, trying not to cry.

"Maybe you need to get out some. You know, date."

"No thanks."

"Leon has a good paying job, and his parents have money."

"Mamm." Annie hated the whine in her voice, but this was a ridiculous conversation.

"I'm not saying you have to marry the guy. Although if you ever saw the quality in him I do, I believe he'd make a good husband. But all I'm trying to tell you is that he has the money to make dating him a fun experience. Nice dinners. Day trips into the city. Time on their horse farm." Her mother shrugged and grabbed another wet towel. "Could be fun and help you not hurt so much, but it's up to you."

Annie passed her a clothespin, appreciating her mother's moment of outreach. "I'll give Leon another try."

Nineteen

Roman counted out change for the last customer paying his bill. "I hope you enjoyed your meal."

"Actually," the man said quietly, "my grilled sandwich was a little burned, and my wife's spoon was dirty."

"I'm so sorry. You should've said something. I'd have been happy to—"

"No problem. She didn't use her spoon. And to be honest, I'm used to slightly burned sandwiches." He shrugged. "Just not from here."

"Well, next time you're in, dessert's on the house."

"I appreciate that, but it's not necessary. Really." He pocketed his change and joined his family.

"I hope you have a happy Mother's Day tomorrow," Roman called to the woman, who smiled as she ushered her four little children out the door.

After turning the Open sign to Closed, he rolled through the dining area, clearing tables. Since Annie had gone back to New York, his brother's mind was always elsewhere.

Not wanting to ponder that any further, Roman thought about the gift he'd ordered for his mom: a porcelain teapot, white with tiny blue roses. The store owner had assured him it would come in today. As soon as he and Aden cleaned up here, he'd head over there to pick it up.

A loud, metallic crash from the kitchen startled him. What on earth?

When he reached the kitchen, he saw an empty busboy bin on the floor with dirty plates, cups, and silverware strewed everywhere. Aden's face was red, and his lips were pressed together as he dumped the items into the bin.

"What happened?"

Aden shrugged.

"Let me guess. You weren't paying attention to what you were doing. Big surprise there."

Aden continued tossing dirty flatware into the bin.

Roman moved closer. "You want to talk about it?"

"Nothing to s-say that you d-don't already know." Aden moved the now-full bin into the sink.

While Annie was here, Aden's stuttering had diminished. Since she'd been gone, it had gotten much worse. Usually Aden stuttered less when he was angry. Now it was more pronounced than ever.

"I c-can't work here any-m-more."

"Don't be ridiculous. What are you going to do?"

Aden didn't nod or shrug or anything. He wasn't asking Roman's opinion. His brother was informing him of the future.

Thoughts of Aden's sketches nagged Roman. "If you're going to leave the diner anyway, why not go after her?"

The taut lines across Aden's face only hinted at all he was thinking as he removed his apron, folded it neatly, and laid it on the counter. "To pr-protect her. Do you understand anything about l-love?"

Roman wanted to, but he always fell so short he made himself sick. Aden's way of handling the situation had left Annie with her family relationships and her reputation intact. She could attend church in New York or here or anywhere else, and people knew nothing about her times of secretly seeing Aden. The few people who were in the restaurant the day her grandfather made a scene thought she had a family emergency and he'd hired a driver to get her home fast. Aden's action would allow her to move on and find a nice Mennonite man and have a family. The Zooks wouldn't lose their diner.

Roman wanted that kind of love in his heart, and despite all the things he'd once had, he'd never had that. Never.

Aden crossed the kitchen and went out the back door.

Roman went after him but had to stop at the doorway. The rocky, washed-out path was not one he could navigate in a wheelchair. "Wait!"

Aden kept going without so much as a glance back at Roman.

"You can't just leave me here!"

Mamm came running in from the dining area. "What is going on in here?"

"He's thrown in the towel and left."

She looked out the back door. "Aden Zook, you get back here

right now," Mamm called. "I need your help getting your brother into the rig."

Roman stared after his brother. Aden had never left the diner without cleaning up, even if he was exhausted or had started running a fever. And he'd never left Roman stranded like this. "Don't worry about it, Mamm. The delivery man will be here later on, and he'll help me get in the rig."

"What just happened in here?"

Roman stared up at his mother. "You know the whole time we were growing up, I had times when I thought I was better than him and he was the unlucky one—that's what I thought. But that's so far from the truth it's scary. Did you know I thought that?"

"I suspected. Even before the accident, insight didn't come easy for you any more than words come easy for Aden."

"Do you think that's why I'm in this contraption now?"

"Like a punishment?" She shook her head. "No, or the whole world would be in one of those. We think too highly of ourselves at some times and too little of ourselves at others. You used to focus on your good attributes and think you were really something. Right now, your biggest obstacle is that you focus only on what you don't have rather than on what you do have. But I'm still praying that you open your heart to God and let Him help you see your life through faith."

Did she see him through faith too? He feared seeing the disappointment in her eyes, so he wouldn't ask that question. "Do you really think Moses would shut us down?"

"Ya, I do."

The question of how she saw him nudged him. "If...you saw me through faith, what would that look like?"

"I see you that way every day. I pray, and I see you whole inside yourself, at peace with your brokenness, and strong enough to be who God called you to be."

"What about Aden and Annie?"

She moved to the kitchen sink. "That's different." Her shoulders slumped. "Ya, it's different," she repeated. "Because it's easier to picture this family through the eyes of faith as long as Moses doesn't shut us down. As long as there's no scandal within the church." She turned to face him. "I mean we can handle everything else, right?"

"I'm confused. Was that sarcasm?"

She straightened her shoulders. "You know what you and I both need? Stronger faith. Somehow we have to rise above our fears... whatever that means."

Roman knew one thing it meant: Mamm would be in the garden for the next five to six months, praying for hours while planting, weeding, and harvesting. He drew a deep breath, feeling strengthened by her honesty. "I think a mom like you deserves to have Mother's Day a lot more than once a year."

"Me too." She sounded half sincere and half sarcastic.

Roman realized that he and his mom were a lot more alike than he'd noticed before, except she held on tight to her beliefs in God's goodness, and he tended to shove God away scornfully. To think that so blatantly was scary. He supposed it was a good thing God was patient.

Twenty

Aden shoved his clothes into a tote bag. Since Annie had returned to New York six weeks ago, every minute here in Apple Ridge was spent wishing things were different. He walked the orchard every night, hoping she'd return.

And fearing she would.

Aden pulled a stack of sketch pads out of the trunk and put them on top of his clothing in the leather tote bag.

The bedroom door opened, and Aden turned. Roman came partway into the room and stopped, studying Aden and his lone piece of luggage.

Aden went into the bathroom and loaded a small vinyl case with his toiletries. When he came back into the bedroom, he walked to his bed without a glance at Roman.

"Where…" Roman clenched the hand rims of his chair. "Where will you go?"

Aden shoved the small bag into the larger one. "Ernie's."

"You won't be happy working on a farm."

"I'm not l-looking to be happy."

Roman stared at the bed. "I know you're still mad at me, but I did what I did to keep from losing you as my helper. To try to hold on to my best friend." Roman wheeled closer to his brother. "If I had to do it over again—our whole lives—I'd be a better brother. Forgive me?"

Aden sat on his bed, staring at the floor. "Ya."

It wasn't like the canyon between Aden and Annie was Roman's fault. When it came to being decisive with Annie, Aden had drifted on floodwaters, hoping for the best but not trying to navigate them at all. "She's b-better off this way."

"That's what you've always thought, isn't it? I mean, it's what kept you from ever writing to her or calling or going to see her at Moses's when she'd come in from New York."

"I never wanted anyone to g-get hurt, Annie m-most of all."

"But over the years when she'd be here visiting and would come into the diner, I always saw that spark between you two. It used to worry me or make me mad." Roman rested a hand on Aden's knee. "Maybe I'm crazy for saying it, but you shouldn't go to Ernie's." Roman rolled his chair back. "You should go to Annie."

Aden couldn't believe his ears. He expected Roman to console him about why keeping a distance was the only nondestructive way to go.

"Ya, Aden, don't listen to me. What do I know? For that matter, what does Moses or Mamm or Daed know? Every one of us is wringing our hands and being selfish. If Annie feels the same way as you do, then together you will find a way to make things work, at least between the two of you."

Aden shook his head. "You're being ri-ri—"

"I'm not being ridiculous. Look, do you think this relationship is wrong?"

"N-no."

"Your feelings for Annie aren't borne from rebellion or sowing wild oats, right?"

Aden rolled his eyes. "No."

Roman grinned. "I'm ready to do whatever I can to convince the family and the community to accept your relationship. And you know I have the gift of being able to talk just about anybody into just about anything."

Aden hadn't done right by Annie. She hadn't wanted to talk about the realities facing them, and Aden hadn't been willing to warn her of the storm that was brewing, and the whole time they were seeing each other, he wavered in where they were heading. Unsure if they'd ever find answers. And unwilling to stop seeing her.

He didn't consider that behavior worthy of her. Aden stood. "I n-need to go."

"You can do this." Roman motioned to the bedroom door. "Go straighten this out. Build a life with her."

"It's d-done. I made sure of it."

"Okay, so you're unsure how you'd convince her of your love. I get that." Roman went closer to the bed and grabbed Aden's tote bag that lay open and pulled out several of the sketchbooks. Aden's eyes widened in surprise. "Show Annie these. They are enough to convince the coldest of hearts." He placed the sketch pads in Aden's lap. "Trust me."

Aden trudged through the woods, following the path to Moses's house. He rehearsed in his mind the words he wanted to say, hoping he could at least get out a few of the sentences.

As he knocked on the front door, he focused on the opening lines he'd spent most of the day planning. But no one came to the door.

Was Moses on a delivery? It seemed unlikely on a Saturday at four o'clock.

Not about to give up, Aden searched the grounds and found Moses in one of the pastures out back. Aden strode that direction, still singing his introductory comments in his head.

When he neared Moses, the older man entered a chicken coop. Aden followed.

Moses dumped two scoops of feed into a plastic container. "You got something on your mind, boy?"

The hymn Aden had chosen to put his words to played in his mind, calming his soul. "I need to t-talk to you about Annie." There. He'd done it. Said a complete sentence with only a single stutter.

Moses walked outside again, and so did Aden. Moses scattered handfuls of feed onto the ground, which the hens and roosters scrabbled over.

Aden waited, trying to gather his thoughts. He prayed.

Moses tossed the buckets inside and dusted his hands together. "You came by here two months ago, saying you were going to do right by her, which we both knew meant you'd end things. But you didn't do that, did you?"

The Scent of Cherry Blossoms

"I intended to, but I c-couldn't."

"I know this is tough. I really do. But here's the way it is, Aden. I'm not interested in anything you have to say about Annie. You leave my granddaughter alone. Completely alone."

The tap-tap-tapping of a woodpecker echoed from a nearby patch of woods. Aden tried to ignore the distracting sound. "I love her. And I'm willing t-to wait for her until you can accept this relationship, like you d-did with Esther."

Moses blinked, apparently surprised Aden knew about that. "Is that so?"

"A-absolutely." Aden needed Moses to understand that this wasn't some heated passion that couldn't be controlled. It was love—the kind that would sacrifice whatever was needed.

"You have no idea the kind of stress your relationship would put on both families."

The woodpecker's tapping began again. This time Aden used its cadence to keep time with the music he'd chosen to think about during this part of his speech. "And I'm s-sorry. It'll be bad, and maybe Annie isn't willing to go through that for us."

"You two haven't made plans behind my back?"

"N-no."

"No strolling arm in arm, making out, or creating a bed out here in the orchard?"

"No sir."

Moses sighed. "You sure don't make it easy for a man to dislike you."

The woodpecker's drumming stopped. Moses started walking

-175-

toward the house, and Aden walked with him. "She knelt before God and gave her word."

"And I won't ask her to br-break it."

"You'll join her faith?"

"N-not because I believe it's more right. B-both groups are right on certain things and wrong on others."

"Your family can't run that restaurant without you. Just do everyone a favor and stay away from Annie." He said it as if those last four words finalized the discussion.

"I c-can't…unless that's what *she* wants."

Halfway up the steps of his home, Moses stopped. "I forbid you. Do you understand me, Aden Zook?"

"W-why?"

Moses went inside, snatched his Bible off the kitchen table, and waved it at Aden. "Because it's wrong! It says not to be unequally yoked!"

Aden studied him, wondering if Moses really thought two Plain believers who'd grown up in a similar manner were unequally yoked. If he had Roman's gift of speaking, he might stand a chance at reasoning with Moses. "I'm s-sorry you feel that way." Aden went out the door he'd just entered. "Denki."

Moses grabbed the door before Aden shut it. "After all I've done for your family, you'll do this to me?"

"It's n-not about you. *Any* of you."

Moses's eyes took on a faraway look, and Aden saw pain and confusion on his withered face. He ran his hand over the worn-out leather Bible before returning to the table.

Moses sat down, saying nothing as Aden continued to wait by the doorway. Moses buried his head in his hands. "I'm not saying I think you're right, but trying to make people do what I think is right hasn't worked either."

Aden blinked. He knew Moses couldn't give his permission outright for Aden and Annie to be together. But it sure sounded as if he was getting awfully close to accepting their relationship.

"You have integrity." Moses got up and began fixing coffee. "Here's my final word, Aden. You pray before you decide what to do about Annie. Talk to God. Be sure you take into account all that she will face. You do that, and I'll not stand in your way, no matter what you decide or who chooses to join which faith."

Aden's heart raced like a wild bird set free of its cage. His lack of words seemed to have allowed Moses to talk until he found the answers Aden needed him to find.

Moses poured water into the coffee maker. "What kind of a man would threaten to remove food out of the mouths of a good woman, her children, and two injured men?"

Aden hoped Moses's words meant he wouldn't pull his partnership from the diner. Roman was wrong that the diner couldn't be run without Aden. It'd need modifications, but Roman had capabilities he never used. Aden would miss the diner but not anything like he'd miss Annie. Other diners could be opened. They wouldn't be a part of him like this one was, but that didn't matter.

All that mattered was Annie...if she'd have him.

Twenty-One

*A*nnie let her little sister run a brush through her hair.

"You have the most beautiful blond hair of any of us," Erla said.

"Denki. But the color of one's hair doesn't matter, my sweet, sweet Erla." Annie tugged on her sister's sleeve. "How about if we have a picnic in our beds after everyone goes home tonight?"

"Ach, Ich lieb sell."

Annie grinned, enjoying her sister's renewed effort to use Pennsylvania Dutch. "I'd love that too."

To appease her mother—and to take a step toward finding some happiness—Annie had agreed to host a couples' gathering in the hangout room above the carriage house. It was just an evening of friends with their dates. They'd play games and talk and eat snacks. Nothing big, but Mamm sure was happy that she'd agreed to it.

Leon would be her date again. He wasn't nearly as boring as she'd once thought. His parents owned several older racing horses, and he'd offered to take her on a ride sometime. She'd always loved horses, and their thoroughbreds were stunning.

"Knock, knock." Mamm tapped on the door while saying the words.

"*Kumm rei.*"

"You're not ready?"

Annie had dawdled for too long, trying to put off the inevitable.

"It's my fault," Erla said.

Annie twisted her hair into a bun and slid hairpins into it. "I'm almost done."

Her mother placed her prayer Kapp onto her head and pinned it into place. "I've made popcorn balls for you to take up to the hang-out room."

"Denki."

The sounds of a carriage outside made her mother gasp. "Your first guest must be here." She went to the window to look out. "Ya. It's Leon. Go." Her mother shooed her out the door. "Don't forget the popcorn balls. I already took drinks and brownies up there."

Annie winked at Erla. "You'll wait up for me tonight?"

Erla nodded.

Annie hurried down the steps and greeted Leon. He helped her tote items up the steps to the carriage room, and within forty minutes they'd greeted numerous guests. The guys and girls sat around on the old furniture and beanbags, eating and talking.

Annie rocked back in a recliner, finally enjoying a reprieve from the weeks of heartache. Leon sat on a stool beside her. He reached behind him and grabbed a deck of cards. "Care to play a game of Dutch Blitz?"

"We'd need two decks if everyone wants to play."

He reached into his shirt pocket and pulled out another pack. "After how much we loved our game the other night, you won't find me without a deck in my pocket."

She laughed. They had enjoyed their time, mostly because his sister was a jokester who kept harassing him the whole time. "Then I do care to play…and win."

"That remains to be seen." While everyone who wanted to play gathered around a huge table, Annie shuffled the cards.

A knock at the door barely registered as Annie dealt cards, turning all of Leon's face up.

He frowned and shoved his cards in front of her and stole her stash.

"No!" Annie laughed and tried to grab her cards back.

"Annie," a girl's voice grabbed her attention.

"Ya?" When she looked up, she saw Aden holding a rather tattered cardboard box with a ribbon around it.

Her thoughts ran crazy, and she imagined tripping over her own feet or blurting out random questions. But she slowly stood. "Excuse me for a minute." She passed the rest of the deck to Leon and went to Aden, gesturing for them to go outside. She stepped onto the landing and closed the door behind her. "What are you doing here?"

"I sent him up there," Erla said. "Is it okay?"

She glanced at the bottom of the stairs. "Ya, Erla. Denki."

Erla waved and headed back to the house.

Why was he in New York?

He held the box out to her. "I m-miss you. And I should have b-boldly told you all I was willing to do to k-keep you in my life."

Annie's heart caught in her throat. She untied the box and opened it. The porch light seemed to offer more shadows than light, but when she looked inside, she saw a stack of sketch pads in various shapes, colors, and sizes. She took out the top one and opened the cover.

In an instant she forgot all about her surroundings—the porch, her friends, and her date with Leon. Aden's drawings immediately transported her back to Apple Ridge, to her grandfather's orchard. To their late-night walks in the moonlight or fog, talking about everything except their future.

When she'd finished looking at the first book, he urged her to open the next. She moved to the top step and sat. He put the box nearby and sat beside her. To her shock it was filled with sketches of her. In the diner's kitchen with her hair a mess, sweeping the floor. In the serving area, her arms loaded with plates as she approached a family at a table. Several were from years ago—events she'd forgotten about. Her in Ellen's garden, kneeling in the dirt, smudges on her cheeks. Roller-skating through the diner. Walking in the rain.

Several pages showed her in her Daadi's orchard, standing among the barren trees, wandering among the budding twigs, touching the blossoms, holding her arms out wide amid an expanse of flowering branches. Every picture portrayed her with a smile on her lips and a glow on her face.

She'd never been that happy unless she was in Apple Ridge with Aden. Not even close. Tears stung her eyes.

Aden smiled. "The d-decision is yours. But, Annie…" He looked into her eyes, silently telling her everything she needed to hear.

Every ounce of love she'd felt for him came rushing back all at once in a torrent of emotion. But every logical reason she'd had for keeping her distance from him came back as well. "But if we do this, your family will lose their livelihood."

"I t-talked to Moses. He's r-relented." He took her hand into his. "But what do you want?"

Her head swam in confusion. She'd spent the last month and a half convincing herself that she was doing the right thing to stay here and that Aden didn't love her. That their feelings for each other were simply childhood affection, not something that could sustain a lasting, happy marriage.

And her relationship with her mother was just starting to mend. Finally, after all these years, they'd actually been able to enjoy each other's company lately. She couldn't risk shattering that.

She stared at the open book in her lap. Only a man who loved her as much as she did him could've drawn those sketches with such detail, precision, and passion.

The door to the carriage house opened, and Leon stepped outside. "Everything okay?"

"Ya." Annie pulled her hand free of Aden's and closed the sketch pad. "I'll just be another minute."

Leon didn't budge.

"Leon, I'll be right in."

He clicked his tongue and went inside.

"I'm sorry, Aden." She rose. "But I have a date for the evening."

"I u-understand." He stood and started to leave but stopped on the stairs and looked back. "I've t-told you what's on my heart. I want to be with you. I'll move here and join your church. The decision is up t-to you."

She watched as he strode to the vehicle he'd apparently arrived in. Before he got in on the passenger's side, he paused, looking at her one last time.

Roman paced the front porch, rolling from one end to the other, waiting on Aden's driver to return. He even managed a few prayers, hopeful God would hear him more this time than He had after the accident.

A desperate feeling gnawed at him, as if life could be set right if Annie agreed to marry Aden and nothing would be set right if she refused him. His eyes stung as tears threatened. Did Aden know how much he admired him? loved him? wanted him to be happy?

Probably not. Roman hadn't even known until recently. From inside the house, Mamm stepped to the screen door. "In diner lingo, the dishes are done, the food is stored away, and I'm about to put the Closed sign on the kitchen for the night. Since you didn't eat supper, you want me to fix you something first?"

Roman shook his head. "What if this doesn't work out but it would have if I'd been the brother I should've been, helping instead of thwarting? That's who Aden's always been to me. But not me. No way. I mean, I'm the smooth talker who just has to push for his way and knows how to do it, right?"

Mamm stepped onto the porch. The screen door slowly squeaked its familiar tune, and when she released it, it banged numerous times against the frame. What was wrong with him that he'd begun noticing the weirdest things and was being moved by them? The sound stirred him, feeling like home, and thankfulness wanted to rise instead of sarcasm.

"Is that where he's gone, to see Annie?"

Roman cleared his throat. "The problem with being a talker is one often doesn't realize what all he's sharing until it's too late."

She sat in the porch swing, staring out over the land. "I'm glad for him."

"We'll be okay, Mamm. I've been thinking a lot lately, driving myself half crazy. But I've finally realized a few things. I'm not as incapable as I make myself out to be. I have limitations, but I became hostile, thinking everyone owed me. I don't want to be that person anymore. I've decided to become determined and find answers…if God will help me."

She smiled. "He will. Come what may, He is there helping, strengthening, and guiding."

"When I stop railing at Him, I actually catch glimpses of different kinds of healing—like accepting the brokenness in my body and trusting Him anyway."

Mamm brushed a stray hair off her forehead and tucked it under her prayer Kapp, and he noticed how much gray hair she had these days. "And, Roman, remember that no one is truly broken whose mind, heart, and soul have been healed by his Creator."

He sort of got that. Everything physical was temporal anyway, and

the most lasting thing people gave each other was who they were…
which was nothing good without God working in them.

Mamm reached over and patted his shoulder. "I guess something
in all this, aside from God's intervention, has been good for you."

"I'd say it's been Marian."

Mamm suppressed a smile as if afraid to look too pleased.

"Get that gleam out of your eye. It's not like that. I'm not getting
any closer to Marian than an occasional phone call. There is no way
I'll ever ask someone with as promising a future as Marian's to hitch
her life to me with my challenges. Forget it."

"You know"—Mamm pressed her hands down the front of her
black apron—"if this works out for Annie and Aden, they face a tough
road ahead: people frowning, one of them being excommunicated, the
other being considered an outsider to the new faith they join. Prejudices will abound for years to come—all of it quite challenging for
them. Right?"

"Aden's worth it. Annie will be the one to miss out if she doesn't
face that challenge."

She leaned toward him. "And I'm here to tell you that the same is
true of Marian." She stood. "Tell me you'll think about that."

He scratched his forehead, a bit rattled by his Mamm's unwaver-
ing belief in him. "I'll call her…see if she might be willing to have a
second date."

"Good idea." She pointed at the road. "But right now, Aden's
home."

Twenty-Two

*I*n the haze between asleep and awake, the scent of cherry blossoms filled Aden's senses. He'd been dreaming about walking through the orchard with Annie in the moonlight. Though he knew it was time to get up, he resisted leaving that precious dream world in which nothing mattered but the love they shared.

As he forced himself to open his eyes, he realized that it was daylight and that the aroma he'd thought was part of his dream still hung in the air. It was a between Sunday, which meant a complete day off. A day to sleep until daylight...or until midmorning if his body ever let him, which it never did.

He got up and dressed, but the aroma of cherry blossoms continued to linger.

That made no sense. He lived too far from Moses's orchard to smell the cherry trees even when they were in full bloom, which they weren't anymore. Was his mind playing tricks on him?

He tried to slip out of the room without waking Roman, but his brother stirred. "Hey, take this with you." Roman pointed to his nightstand where a box sat, wrapped in forest-green paper with navy-blue ribbon and a small bow. The square of white cardboard taped to the top said, "With love, from Roman and Aden."

Suddenly it hit Aden that today was Mother's Day! He'd been so wrapped up in his feelings about Annie he hadn't thought to get his Mamm a present.

"Y-you—"

"I know." Roman scrunched his pillow under his head. "You think I should give it to her. But I want to sleep, and she deserves to know first thing that we thought of her." He snuggled into the pillow. "Or at least the best one of us did."

Aden chuckled, so grateful his brother was more like himself again. Carrying the present, he closed the door behind him. While heading for the kitchen, he also smelled coffee and fresh-baked cinnamon rolls. When he entered the room, he nearly dropped his mother's present.

Annie sat at the kitchen table with his mom, sipping coffee. Mamm looked peaceful and happy for the first time in weeks, maybe a month or more. Apparently, between when he left her last night and this morning, Annie had hired or bartered with a driver to bring her here.

"Good morning, Son." Mamm rose and gave him a kiss on the cheek. "Is that for me?"

Aden tore his attention from Annie and extended the gift. "Ya. Happy Mother's Day."

"Why, thank you."

"It's from Roman and me. Mostly Roman."

"Then I'll wait till he gets up to open it." She set it in the center of the kitchen table.

"Good morning, Aden." Annie smiled up at him, looking so beautiful.

"Annie brought me a gift too." Mamm took his hand and led him to the living room. "Candles with the scent of cherry blossoms." The two large candles were lit and filled the room with the fragrance that would always remind Aden of the girl he loved.

Annie came up behind them. "If you're not too hungry, maybe we could go for a walk?"

He studied her face, longing to tell her that he was more hungry for her than for any kind of food. But she still hadn't told him how she felt—at least not in words. Her presence here, and the sparkle in her eyes when she looked at him, gave him hope.

"I have a gift for you, Aden."

When they stepped out the back door, he saw a root-wrapped sapling in the corner of the porch. Annie picked it up and handed it to him. "I went by a garden center late last night, not expecting them to be open or to have what I wanted. I was wrong on both counts. This little cherry tree is just a sapling. But it comes from good stock, so it should grow big and strong and yield abundant, fragrant blossoms, given the proper care."

As he took the young tree from her, his fingers brushed hers, and he let them linger there. "And w-where will we plant it?"

The look in her eyes told him she heard his underlying question. "I've given that a lot of thought, and I have an idea." She led him across the backyard to a large, relatively flat area. "Seems to me this might be a good place for a cherry tree. There's lots of room, and it'll get plenty of sunshine. And it'll be near our home."

Aden looked across the land, hoping he wasn't about to wake up. He set the cherry tree on the ground.

Annie knelt and wrote his name in the topsoil. "I spoke to my mother about us."

Aden crouched beside her. "H-how did it g-go?"

She raised her eyes to Aden's. "She said that love and loyalty are worth sacrificing for and our people know that. In time your people and mine will forgive us for ruffling their feathers." The dimple in her right cheek grew clear as she smiled. "I want to join your family, Aden. I want to be a part of your life here with Ellen and Roman and the diner."

Aden took her by the hand and helped her stand. He tucked a loose strand of her silky blond hair behind her ear and gazed into her bluish-green eyes. "I love you, Annie Martin."

<hr/>

Roman sat at the breakfast table with his family and Annie. It was a nice start to Mother's Day. But he knew that by tomorrow, Annie's church leaders, both from New York and here in Apple Ridge, would counsel and pressure her not to leave the church, and when she didn't relent, she'd be shunned. The Mennonite community didn't call it that. He didn't know what they called it, but it carried the same shame and sense of isolation, only, unlike the Amish, there would be no set time for when it'd end. Loved ones and church members would turn a cold, disapproving shoulder to her, and she could face that discord from her people for years, and maybe from some for a lifetime.

Little would change in their household. The Amish church leaders would speak with her, caution her, and once they trusted her decision was based on love, they'd begin the steps of welcoming her.

But Roman would never let himself forget the sacrifice or the hurt she was going through. He'd be her friend in every way possible, going the extra mile to be kind and supportive.

The phone rang, and he dropped his fork. He'd called Marian last night. A sibling answered, saying she was out. He said he would call back and asked that no one pick up the phone so he could leave her a voice mail with a very specific message: "If you are willing to give me another chance, another date, please call."

He backed up from the table and wheeled through the house, down the ramp, and into the phone shanty as fast as he could. He jerked up the phone. "Hello."

"Friends may come and go, but enemies tend to accumulate." Marian's voice washed over him.

He laughed. "Experience is what you get when you didn't get what you wanted."

"So what do you want, Roman?"

"A chance with you, Marian."

She didn't respond, and he did the one thing that never came easy—kept his mouth shut and waited.

"Roman," she finally said, and he noted that seriousness had replaced the humor in her voice. "It was always yours for the asking."

Acknowledgments

To my wonderful big brother Mark—no matter how young or old we are, you always make time for your little sister. Thank you for sharing your expertise about repairing generators! You are endlessly patient with my lack of understanding when it comes to all things mechanical.

To my dear Old Order Amish friends—you always have more answers than I have questions. (And that's quite a feat!) Thank you for your friendship and for every invitation to stay in your homes. Time with you, whether on the phone or in person, inspires and encourages me in every way imaginable. Your inside view of Old Order Amish life and "Zook's Diner" made writing this book a joy. No matter what I needed—answers, recipes, a seamstress to make clothes for the cover model, a place to stay, or firsthand experience of Zook's Diner—you had a solution. I can't thank you enough!

A special thank-you to several new friends—both current and former horse-and-buggy Mennonites—all of whom wish to remain anonymous. You willingly invested in this story and in me. Without that gift to me, the authenticity of this story would be compromised.

Always close to my heart are the folks at WaterBrook Multnomah. From marketing to sales to production to editorial—thank you! No matter what challenges arise, you meet them with wisdom and grace.

And to my wonderful family. You are everything I need and more.